THE JOB

THE JOB

IRENE DISCHE

BLOOMSBURY

First published in Great Britain 2002
This paperback edition published 2003

Copyright © 2000 by Irene Dische

Originally published in 2000 as *Ein Job* by Hoffmann und Campe, Hamburg
Based on a film idea by Nizamettin Aric and Irene Dische

The moral right of the author has been asserted

Bloomsbury Publishing Plc, 38 Soho Square, London W1D 3HB

A CIP catalogue record for this book
is available from the British Library

ISBN 0 7475 6166 4

10 9 8 7 6 5 4 3 2 1

All papers used by Bloomsbury Publishing are natural,
recyclable products made from wood grown in sustainable,
well-managed forests. The manufacturing processes
conform to the environmental regulations of the
country of origin.

Typeset by Hewer Text Ltd, Edinburgh
Printed by Clays Ltd, St Ives plc

www.bloomsbury.com/irenedische

This is a true story. I will call it:

THE JOB

THE ASSASSIN BEGAN HIS career throwing snowballs. His first targets were the green legs and squeaking boots of the soldiers that patrolled his Kurdish town in eastern Turkey. The assassin was cautious, his aim poor. He was just a first-grader. After the Turkish soldiers beat up his father (the merchant had refused to salute when the police band played the national anthem) he perfected his craft. He packed his snowballs tightly, warmed them in his bare hands and let them freeze again to glaze them with ice. His palms were always red and chapped.

As the assassin's aim improved, so did his enjoyment. His ferocity set in like a sudden fever at dusk, after a day of cold docility at school, where he was learning to speak Turkish, learning the history of Turkish accomplishments, Turkish poetry, the geography of Turkish expansionism through Europe. His teachers succeeded in beating the Kurdish accent out of him cleanly, giving him an advantage in his future profession. He was polite, obedient, used to hearing

1

compliments about his pretty face, and lazy about his lessons. His ambitions lay elsewhere. He studied the Turkish soldiers, their handsome green outfits, the rifles they used as truncheons. He found he could not distinguish among these figurines. So he stopped concentrating on their legs, and aimed instead for their faces. Then he could identify them, and check the degree of injury he had inflicted.

One winter afternoon, when his comrades had already gone home, the assassin decided to patrol the area one more time. He crept along the snow-covered roofs of the houses, jumping from one to the next, a canvas bag filled with snowballs hanging from his shoulder. He made his way quickly through the village. But it was late, it was getting dark, it was slippery, and he misjudged the distance from one roof to the next. Instead of landing safely on the far side, he pitched forwards, head first, into an embankment of powdered snow. He felt himself glide downwards. He struggled. But his frantic movements only made him slide further down. The snow scalded him. Time slowed, and he felt inclined to say something. He opened his mouth to speak. Snow pushing down his throat made him gag on the phrase: 'Goodbye, Grandmother!'

Suddenly he felt a vice tighten on one foot, then on the other. His burning body stabilized. It began to move upwards again. He was hauled skywards. He recalled how he had called to his grandmother, and the relief he felt was cancelled by a much stronger emotion: he wept with embarrassment. He wiped his eyes with a new kind of panic as he travelled and saw a brown leather boot, and a green leg.

2

'Where do you live?' asked a voice.

He was hanging upside down, both his feet encased in the massive grip of a soldier's fist. Shame upon shame. Although he knew he had the pose of a trapped rabbit, he answered the soldier's question, pointing his frozen little index finger at the very last house on the road. The soldier carried his trophy by its feet, clad in rubber boots made from an old tyre, to the outskirts of the village. The assassin's grandmother was waiting anxiously in the doorway, and began her howl of relief from afar. The soldier handed the child over the threshold.

'I found this in a snow bank. I guess it's still alive,' he said.

To the assassin's amazement, his grandmother asked the soldier inside, covered his gloved hands with kisses, and insisted he drink a glass of tea and eat some fresh bread. The next day, the assassin was back on his post. This time he inserted a stone into each snowball before applying saliva and pressing the mass tight. He had found his calling.

ONE

IN THE WINTER OF the Kurdish year 2603, that is, some years before the third Christian millennium, when Alan was a man with faith only in himself and his ability to be heartless, he arrived in New York City on a plane from Frankfurt. I hope you'll never need to go to New York, because it's a colony of creepy, crawling, nameless inhabitants, none of whom speak good English, the way you or I do. Alan saw his degradation as he entered the emigration hall, it was written on the wall, advertised: posters hung there, showing unnaturally beautiful people doing the most natural things, brushing their teeth or eating a hamburger. Alan felt ashamed of himself right away: he was no longer as young, no longer as handsome. In that tired, poor state of mind, he reached the first hurdle, the passport controls.

He did not draw attention to himself there. It can be said about him, as a rule, that those who didn't recognize him never noticed him; he passed by with all the fanfare of a shadow. Everything about him was sombre, from his stiff woollen coat to the features of his face – *hila hila!*: he looked unusual. His eyes were black as damp earth, his two-day beard had precise contours, dividing his face neatly into light and dark, into above and below. His nose, mouth and chin were as chiselled and evenly spaced as the tombstones in a well-kept graveyard. But an observer's attention never settled there, because an expression of reserve deflected even casual curiosity. Alan arrived in America nearly empty-handed, carrying only a plastic bag of duty-free cigarettes. His pockets did not weigh him down – they were empty except for a brand-new German passport. This precious document aroused no admiration in the American official, not even suspicion.

This magistrate glanced at the passport photo and clapped the green covers together in one motion, grumbling, 'Welcome to the United States.' He consulted his watch; it was nearly lunchtime.

Alan continued towards the exit, passing by the luggage belts. He shuddered to see what was going on there, the manner in which this system treated all possessions as equal. So it was a good thing, after all, that he had been unable to subject his kidskin leather suitcase, with the red silk lining, to democracy. When the door to the arrivals hall opened, he saw the masses of people staring in his direction from behind a barrier. But this crowd, unlike others he had recently encountered, ignored him. He pressed ahead.

A cluster of men separated from the others and marched towards him.

One spoke in Kurdish, 'Hello there, come this way.'

Several torsos puffed up by ski parkas surrounded him, led him outside, into the cold. No one spoke, but swinging arms and striding legs whisked him along. A yellow car was waiting at the kerb. A large but vulgar car. The back door swung open. He climbed in, settled his bag of cigarettes on the ugly fabric, and sat again, as he had for the past days. He disliked this position – he considered sitting the pose of boredom and constraint. One of his new companions sat down next to him in the back seat and unfurled a Turkish newspaper under his nose, which featured a front-page photo of the Black Stone.

Alan was not a practised reader. He read the article aloud, peering with interest at the photo, his voice expressionless – the news that the Black Stone, a notorious assassin, had escaped from the central Istanbul prison, in a daring coup, shortly after a Turkish tribunal had convicted him for the premeditated murder of a Turkish businessman, and sentenced him to life in jail.

'They give you credit for everything!' said his neighbour, while the driver wrenched the key in the ignition, and pulled the car away from the kerb.

'It is an old photo. They never could get a newer one,' Alan said. Then he added bitterly, 'I sure had a lot of hair then.'

'And that terrific moustache. In America you can get yourself new hair. You can get anything here for money,' said his neighbour, removing his parka, revealing a Dormeuil pinstripe double-breasted suit. One cuff button stood open, displaying a hand-sewn buttonhole. He switched easily between English, when addressing the others, and Kurmanci, the Kurdish that Alan spoke. 'And in America you can get money if you work hard. So you're lucky. We have work for you. You have a chance to prove yourself. One chance. Do it right, you're a free man. Make a mistake then you're back in Istanbul being tortured to death. We needed someone special for the job. You're special.' The car lurched into traffic. 'I promised the others we'd have some fun watching you work. Do you think so?' Alan shrugged. His neighbour bestowed upon Alan the carniverous smile of the do-gooder, and said, 'We'll give you a few days to get settled. If you feel funny, don't worry. That's jet lag. And now – look around you. This here is the land of the free.' He gestured at the murky straits of Queens outside the car window.

'It's all yours,' he went on. 'Including an apartment in a pleasant neighbourhood. An American passport. Freedom of this and that. Whatever job you like. At a small price. Incidentally, my name is Mr Ballinger. Pleased to meet you at last. May I introduce the driver, and my other friend up front – I won't bother you with their names, they're not going to become your companions the way I am.'

'The terms?' asked Alan, turning the knives of his gaze directly towards Mr Ballinger. But the American was not intimidated.

'An assignment, pretty routine. You've done this sort of thing before.'

'I don't speak a word of English, you know that.'

'Of course. We know everything, *canê*.'

Canê means darling in Kurdish. Alan felt insulted by the intimacy. But he was unarmed, and couldn't show it.

'What's my name, anyway,' he asked, finding his composure in the patience that had grown over his dead heart. He noticed similar yellow cars on the road, with passengers in the back seat.

'The same. Alan. Mem Alan was King of the Kurds. But Alan is also a good American name. Last name will be Korkunc. You were born in Ankara. You have a degree in business administration from Ankara University. And a job in a textile firm. You better give me that German passport – it can only get you in trouble.'

Alan handed it to him reluctantly.

'We're going to bring you to an apartment now. It's pretty far from your job, but you'll get the hang of driving here. I have a weak spot for this neighbourhood, and the apartment has such a nice view. This car is yours until you've finished.'

'This car!' he protested. 'It's a taxi.' A chevy. With cheap seat covers and a plastic console. He had never driven anything but Mercedes.

'That's right,' said Mr Ballinger. 'People who can't speak English drive taxis in New York.'

He leaned forwards to the men in the front of the car and spoke. Alan heard the thunderclap of their laughter. Unspeakable isolation, when others laugh and you don't understand why.

'I told them at least you have a real driver's licence,' Mr Ballinger explained. 'That's more than this driver ever had. And about your three Mercedes, including a jeep.'

'Your Kurdish is excellent,' said Alan. 'But you are obviously not Kurdish.'

'Not at all. But some Jewish blood,' said Mr Ballinger.

9

He opened his eyes wide, providing blue backdrops for his marauding pupils, and pursed his lips: pride. New York is full of types like that, whose faces are nothing but a showroom floor on which various emotions can be arranged to impress an onlooker. This Mr Ballinger was used to being in control. Even his clothes obeyed him – usually, clothes are in charge of people and not the other way around, but Mr Ballinger's suit draped his chest with real deference, wanted to be of service. Even his blond hair had not abandoned him; although it was fading in colour, it remained provocatively thick. Mr Ballinger added a touch of sadness to his display of pride by lowering his booming baritone.

'Homosexual. An outcast. My great-aunt even died in a concentration camp. That's why I understand the Kurds. I speak all four Kurdish languages. You don't need to know anything about me, but I'll tell you anyway – I'm a linguist. In fact, I've just been elected to the Sentinel Club.'

Alan did not look at him, and did not reply. Some people enjoy the feeling of dislike, but he did not. He would do nearly anything to avoid that sensation.

*   *   *

The late-afternoon sun was putting on a display for the newcomer. Peering to his left as the taxi sped along a highway, he watched the sun set as a slow fireball, the city lying in a grey slag-heap beneath it. Alan judged the car to be travelling northwards along an empty avenue of water on his right that the other passengers referred to as the East River. He treated this information with the interest that a man lost in the wilderness takes in his compass. When the car turned off the highway, he noted that it turned westwards, and southwards again, down a street gaudy with shops and produce, and teeming with English speakers.

'Ever heard of Broadway?' asked Mr Ballinger. 'Well, this is it. You want to speak to anyone, forget English, learn Spanish.'

The cab slowed down on a small street overlooking another river, as wide as the Bosphorus. The sun appeared to have crashed into the water, was coming apart, staining the water deep red. But the sun did this daily in Istanbul, old shenanigans. The taxi pulled into an underground garage, wound downwards, and parked in a spot with a white sign reading 'Reserved Number 45'.

'People kill for parking space here,' warned Mr Ballinger.

His companions looked troubled. They began to converse agitatedly. Alan listened to the soft syllables with amusement. He had never placed much value on conversation, so he didn't mind if it was incomprehensible.

'Crime,' one was saying in a preacher's voice, as he stepped out of the car. He repeated this word several times, and then the others took it up too.

Finally Mr Ballinger roared at them, 'Shut up!' whereupon they all looked cowed, and he lowered his voice, became reasonable again. 'Alan, don't forget your number. Same as your age. I had to fire a gentleman working for me last year who kept parking in the wrong space.'

They headed towards an elevator, but Alan baulked. He mistrusted elevators. They could take him prisoner.

'Let's walk,' he said.

Mr Ballinger translated this, for the amusement of the

others. They humoured him, trudging up a cement stairwell. Upstairs lay a tidy little avenue of red-brick houses festooned with fire escapes. The street lights had already switched on, but they stood far apart, and did little to illuminate the gloom seeping in from the east, from Turkey, where gloom begins.

Mr Ballinger stopped, swept his arm out and announced, 'This is home. Practise that in English: home. Home.' His mouth formed an o and held it as a long note.

Home was a clean, six-storey brick building. Home was on the top floor, and anyone who feared elevators could rest easy, because there wasn't one. Residents had to climb upstairs, listening to their footsteps like a hacking cough in the stairwell. Home had one room with a cot, a shiny black plastic bedside table, worn parquet floors and plaster walls where time had spun a web of cracks. A naked light bulb dangled from the ceiling. The window was sealed by black metal gates – burglar protection. Home had a windowless kitchen with a larger shiny black plastic table, a matching chair, a stove and a quaking refrigerator. Mr Ballinger beckoned the new tenant to take a seat in the kitchen chair. While the others stood in the doorway, Alan complied. He sat down, relaxed, took a pack of cigarettes from his plastic bag and lit up. He puffed instead of inhaling, and the kitchen clouded over.

Mr Ballinger tossed a wallet stuffed with bills on the table, two sets of keys, a piece of paper with a telephone number, a map of Manhattan with a name and an address scrawled on the margin, and a large photograph.

'You can study the photograph. You take care of those people on the photo, and not Mr Erkal, who hangs around with them.

Sulymon Erkal. You know who that is. Ex-governor of Kurdistan. That's your old neighbourhood, I know. When you were a kid you probably hated him. But now, sir, you are all grown-up. A professional man. You can keep your paws off him. It's the others who should interest you. Their address is here. Today is Sunday. Tomorrow, we'll get you some tools of the trade. On Friday afternoon, Sulymon is flying to Istanbul for the weekend. Now listen closely. You have five days to set things up, then you execute the task and leave. No time for play, you work a full week. You'll find that in America people actually enjoy working. Because they want to get ahead of their neighbours. Hey!'

Alan slouched in the chair smoking, his eyes closed throughout Mr Ballinger's speech. Now he allowed his eyelids to drift upwards.

Mr Ballinger spat his p's.

'Pay attention when I speak!' Alan looked at him without interest, but it assuaged the speaker, who resumed in a quiet but commanding tone. 'On Friday afternoon, a limousine picks Sulymon up at home, and that's your cue to go inside the house, with this key here, and look after whoever he left inside. In any way you please. We want to see at least one set of ears as proof. You return them to us with the car keys. Everything else you leave as is – as a surprise to Sulymon when he returns on Monday. And don't get mixed up. We don't want a hair on his head touched, you understand? Nothing. We need him. We need him, but without the delusions of grandeur. We need to pull him down a notch or two. And those people in the picture here, they're what's giving him his backbone and his big mouth.'

13

Alan was not given to surprise or curiosity. He didn't look at the picture.

'It's not a problem,' he said to Mr Ballinger.

'There's a burglar alarm on inside the house. The combination is 1923. Birth year of your republic. They couldn't think of a better one. Use the taxi and the map to get around,' said Mr Ballinger. 'Oh, and your new neighbour here has the same name as you – Allen – but don't let that impress you. You keep to yourself.'

'Another Alan?' he asked, unsettled.

'Yes, sir. But this one is not exactly King of the Kurds, the way you are. This is our guest apartment. I am fond of it, there's a little tickle of danger when I come to visit you. One has to fight routine in every profession. You can handle the neighbourhood, for a few days. We'll get you into another one as soon as you've finished the job. Don't forget, you're a loner. We don't want any trouble with extras. No friends, no floozies, nothing. My company will have to do you. I'll call you from time to time. Or call on you, if things take too long. Here's a telephone. To reach me you press this button. Can you remember that? You have to charge the telephone up with this – oh, you know how these things work?'

Alan was enthusiastic.

'I have one in Istanbul.'

Mr Ballinger corrected him.

'You *had* one in Istanbul. If the phone rings, answer. It's me, and no one else. And we want you available at all times. So take the telephone with you wherever you go, even the bathroom, *canê*.

And then they all took turns staring at him meaningfully, and, one after the other, they switched their torsos about, showing him their backs, and left the little kitchen. Alan heard the front door close softly behind them, their footsteps in the hallway like distant applause.

*   *   *

Later, Alan moved to the bedroom, and sat down on the cot. The springs grunted, speaking the same language as his prison bed in Istanbul. He shifted his weight just to hear them again. No one was watching him, so he had fun. Soon he was bouncing wildly, as high as he could. Then he stopped, and contemplated the absence of motion. He sighed so loudly that the crestfallen prison guards being punished for negligence back home probably overheard him. Well, his feet were aching, and that's something the strongest man can't ignore for long. He bent down and removed his shoes, his favourite pair. He was still wearing the yellow Joop socks an admirer had smuggled into court for him, on his request, and he had worn for his sentencing. He looked at the socks. He had no others. He sighed again, a kind of song – melancholy always wants to sing – and stretched out on his back. He fell asleep instantly like that, his face turned to the ceiling. It grew dark, and the cockroaches came out to play.

He woke up as a blind man. He asked the walls, 'Where do Americans keep their light switches?' The walls guided him to the kitchen. He opened the refrigerator door, and that faint, blessed light inside illuminated the darkness. A string hung from the ceiling. He yanked it, the light bulb overhead went on. The horde of cockroaches dispersed. He watched them without malice. He rubbed his dry eyes, concerned that they looked swollen. The stubble on his face was out of control. For once, he was glad there were no mirrors in the apartment. He took milk, a stick of butter and a loaf of sliced bread from the icebox, and tore open the milk carton, guzzling it straight while his fingers were prising open the bag of bread. He stuffed a slice into his mouth. As he ate, he glanced at the photograph lying on the table. It showed two small girls of perhaps five and seven years, being cuddled by a young woman who was obviously their mother.

He was surprised enough to stop chewing, for an instant. He stood up. This brought him within arm's reach of a cupboard, so he opened it. He found plastic plates, cutlery and Styrofoam cups. He positioned a set formally at the table, sat down again, poured himself milk, and tried to butter the bread. American bread can bring a strong man to his knees. The bread shredded at the touch of the plastic knife. Finally he gave up. He bit directly into the butter, and then into the bread. He had a feast.

*   *   *

A really refreshing nap must be followed by a snack, and a really refreshing snack by a stroll, which can be followed by a snack, and then a nap, and that's the good life. Alan subscribed to this, which meant it was time for a stroll, never mind the hour. Darkness was a familiar landscape to him, the night was really his home. He took to the sidewalks, enjoying the affirmative tap of his footsteps; *hila hila*, he had been able to keep his beloved handmade Hungarian shoes on his feet throughout his custody. It wouldn't be bad to have a second pair.

16

Turning a corner, he reached the main avenue, Broadway. It was a windless night, and the litter lay still, ankle-deep. He felt at ease – Istanbul was just as dirty, just as stagnant. There would be cleaner neighbourhoods. He would move there when the job was finished. He would be rich and beloved here, the way he was in Turkey. Would would would. The future tense can be such a comfort. He came across a glistening lake of light that spilled from a pastry shop. Booths were placed in the window, and he could see the diners, illuminated as if they were on stage. They chewed and slurped. Alan felt in his pockets, fondled the wallet. But his path to the doorway was blocked.

An overcoat stood there, its hem swinging gently around a pair of pleated trouser legs. From a distance of a few feet, the coat looked like a Brioni. No visible seams. But when his gaze sought out the shoes, Alan's assumptions came under attack. The owner's style had a glaring flaw. He had a dog. For professional and aesthetic reasons, Alan despised dogs, and expected others to do the same. This fine man focused all of his attention on a small white terrier crouching on the sidewalk right next to that extraordinary trouser leg. The dog was defecating. He was not good at it. His owner monitored the situation, his face stricken with concern. He spoke softly, urgently. His monologue ended abruptly; he held his breath. Finally, he sighed loudly and said, over and over, 'Gudog!' While the dog turned around and sniffed appreciatively at the fruits of his labour, the man's behaviour became even more bizarre: he stretched a plastic glove over his hand, as if he didn't want to leave fingerprints, and bent down towards the stool. He shook open a plastic bag with his free hand. With his gloved hand, he dropped the stool inside the bag, regarded the brown smear, murmured 'Gudog' and strode to a waste basket, where he deposited it with reluctance and respect, like a housewife throwing away wilted flowers.

Alan did not hesitate: he gave the dog a quick vicious kick in the ribs. He was not struck by a bolt of lightning for this. No signs that any divinity had even noticed. Even the owner sensed no unhappiness – he remained bowed over the garbage. The dog howled and scuttled the length of his leash, but his owner concentrated on the bin. With his way no longer blocked, Alan turned back to the pastry shop, and went inside.

He had seen shops like this in the movies, with plastic booths and clean linoleum. He had never suspected their aroma – of fresh pastry. A waitress dressed in white was leaning on the counter, her face turned downwards to a book with a glossy picture cover. The entering customer noted with pleasure that she was not too thin. He always enjoyed new scenery. A brooch on her lapel read 'Pat'. Alan sauntered over, stared at her *memik*, to show her how much he liked them. Pat straightened up, put the book down. He became confused. He had never looked closely into such a face. She was from Africa. A *kanibal*. *Yam-yam*.

Finally, he spoke to her, with the language he knew.
'*Kahve*.'

She replied, in gibberish.

'OK,' he said, not understanding, not caring.

Women often spoke. He had heard dreadful tales about African habits, but he had seen photographs of naked

African women who had the loveliest fruit. These seemed constrained by baskets that surely included lace. He wondered about their *serimemekin*, their centrepieces. Probably they looked like small hard black stems. He wasn't sure he wanted to get close to them, but he certainly wanted to see them. And the fragrant bush, in her armpits. She was still speaking, her tone seemed inquisitive.

'OK, OK,' he repeated, wishing she would turn around so he could review the rest of her.

Her voice rose slightly. She had to be appeased.

He bared his teeth: he smiled. She poured a cup full with cream, added a little coffee, and pushed it towards him. He pointed again.

'Donut?' she said.

'Do-nut,' he answered. His second English word.

She picked up a jelly donut and spoke on.

Alan produced his wallet, and took out a bill with the number 100 on it. He hoped it was enough.

The bill seemed to annoy her. He stared at her face, a part of the body that he did not usually notice – the crimson, smooth inner side of her dark lower lip aroused his interest. Her nose was wide, but dainty. She was snapping the bill open, holding it to the light. The donut lay on the counter. He knew that he could not take it until the price had been negotiated. He forgot her. He felt the precariousness of his hopes, in the hands of this strange woman. The smell of a fresh donut can turn the biggest man into a trembling, salivating cur.

She held the bill up for all to see, waving it, and calling to them. He could not know why. The other diners looked up, and peered at the bill. Several of them appeared odd, their bodies wider than he had thought possible. He had never seen human beings so fat. The fat man at the Ankara amusement park was not nearly as wide, and he made a living off his unique size. These creatures regarded Alan with curiosity. Their faces were not unfriendly, in fact, they all smiled as they shrugged or shook their heads at him. The waitress handed the bill back to him, muttering something. He turned to leave but she called, 'Hey, mister!' When he looked back at her, she was extending a plate with a donut, and a cup of coffee, and speaking rapidly. He took her offering, nodding his head to show dignified, but not grateful, acceptance.

What she said was, 'Pay me next time. Or you'll burn in hell.'

He took a seat at a booth, inspected the donut before hazarding a bite. He had been right to exercise caution – red jelly squirted into his lap. It reminded him of a job he had once witnessed in Istanbul. He opened his mouth as wide as he could, and stuffed the rest of the pastry inside. Panic about choking gave way to bliss. The other guests watched him with interest. Many had jelly stains on their clothes.

Alan admonished himself that had he eaten more slowly he would be eating still. Greedily, he lit a cigarette.

Instantly, the waitress was standing across from him. He felt pleased. He believed he had drawn her there. A loud voice issued from the void of her face.

'OK,' he replied. He inhaled deeply and squinted upwards at her. This manner of gazing had met with much success in

20

Istanbul when he was trying to make friends. Her arm lashed out. A dark finger with white undersides pointed at the no-smoking sign, and he heard her hiss, 'ṣmuk.'

He didn't know what to make of this. He stared at her mouth, and licked his own lips. A trembling ran through her as she sighed. An arm swung slowly in his direction, until a small hand reached the cigarette clenched between his teeth. He felt it sliding out from between his lips, and caught a glimpse of it dropping into his coffee.

Under the circumstances, he remained gentle. He stood up, backed towards the door, glad that there had been no witnesses from Turkey. If he had looked back, he would have seen Pat behind the counter, opening her shiny book again.

*   *   *

Alan's impression of the first woman he had met in America was the embarrassment she had caused him. Her offence was so horrendous that it confused him, and he could not figure out how to teach her a lesson. He returned to the darkness. But he had little time to enjoy his solitude there, because he recognized a related gait behind him. Soft, shuffling. He slowed down to listen. The footsteps slowed. His pulse sped up. It's one thing to be the target of strangers with evil intentions in a city that you know. It's another in a city you don't know. And it's yet another being the object of anyone's interest whatsoever in New York, whether you know the place or not. I sincerely hope you never do. No city is as sinister. Above Los Angeles or Vegas or Chicago, lie beautiful, spacious skies. And beneath the concrete, there

21

wave amber fields of grain. New York is like an inhabited porous concrete slab. If you lift a corner, you'll find more concrete beneath. There is no air above and no dirt beneath New York City, but concrete that goes all the way to the very centre of the globe. And on his first night in New York, the darkness began to writhe like a monster around him; he was being followed.

He saw no point in trying to evade his pursuer, nor in confronting him. He became passive; he went home. He passed through the lobby quickly, the door slamming behind him, headed for the stairwell, heard the front door open and close again in the lobby again, and the feet following. He started up the stairs. The wind howled in the shaft, 'Who?' and, 'Why?' The footsteps had reached the stairwell, and started their ascent behind him. When Alan reached the sixth-floor landing, he turned into the hall, pressed his back against the wall, and waited. Soon, his tormentor reached the sixth floor, and entered the hallway.

*   *   *

It is not a rare occasion, in Alan's line of work, to be followed. Every job has some negative aspects. Like a physician being exposed to a head cold, Alan did not chafe about the danger, but faced it with dignity. He prepared to fight with his bare hands.

But then, the *falan-filan* who had stalked Alan all the way from Broadway to his own dark front hall, revealed himself, standing before Alan in a pose that demonstrated a contemptible lack of caution, facing Alan's door, his back exposed to any enemy. An amateur. He put his ear against the door. After standing there and listening a while, he straightened up, sighed, a long-drawn-out F followed by a click. Alan understood that – '*Fakabasti!*'. It was one of his favourite expressions too, a cry of success, as triumphant as 'Checkmate!'. But what did this son of a donkey mean, who now heehawed *Fakabasti* at his door? After that, he turned and began tramping downstairs without taking the slightest consideration of any need for secrecy. America! Alan waited till the stairwell had settled into quiet again, and then he went home.

Inside his apartment, that giant, loneliness, waited. Alan fought him with chores. He took off his trousers, and cleaned them with hot water – there was no soap. He succeeded, by dint of scrubbing furiously with his knuckles, in removing the jelly stains. He hung the dripping apparel over a radiator and paced the apartment in his long woollen underwear. He opened the window. The burglar gates proved vulnerable to brute strength – he removed them, throwing them downwards. Instead of tumbling into an abyss, they bounced outside his window. He saw he had a small metal terrace. He crawled through the window, and squatted there, on the fire escape, in what seemed absolute darkness. It was daylight in Istanbul. By rights, he should be eating his first breakfast now, olives and cheese, and some strong coffee, before retiring to his bathroom, where the sun was lighting up the pink marble. But a slip-up had cost him his right to his existence in Istanbul. The cold, his old friend, consoled him, running its fingers through his hair, along his ears, his thighs, and wrapped around his feet. Squatting always made Alan sleepy. He dozed. Once, a light went on in a window that proved to be just a few metres away, and he saw that he was sitting high up in a courtyard. In the apartment across the yard, an old man was using a toilet. When he finished, the light went off. Much later, Alan's telephone rang. He listened to it for a while, before crawling back through the window.

It was Mr Ballinger.

'Just wanted to hear how you were getting on.'

Alan looked at his watch: 3.30 a.m.

'Fine, thank you.'

'I've just had a long evening at the club. I was thinking about taking you there sometime. You should meet some influential people. Would you like that? It's risky for me to be seen with you, but I like a risk. I'm a gambler at heart. And I think I should be a good host.'

When Alan did not reply he said, 'Well, goodnight.'

Alan hung up the phone without speaking. The wind had followed him inside and was swirling around the room. He closed the window, and lay down on the bed. The cockroaches cavorted. A book had been laid on the night table – *Learn English In Six Days*. He did not bother to open it. He thought, Alan does not need to go to English, English will come to Alan. He imagined himself speaking English, rapidly, gesticulating to make a point. It was easy. He heard music through the wall. A woman was singing a wailing Western song. He hummed along making a lot of mistakes – he had never heard Mozart before – until he finally fell asleep.

TWO

ALAN KORKUNC NEEDED AN alarm clock to wake up – it was one of his few weaknesses. When he awoke, it was noon, and the cockroaches had disappeared. He lay in bed for a while, smoking, dropping the ashes on the parquet, wondering about his new life, and singing a Kurdish ballad about a pretty wife who addresses her husband at dawn: Good morning, my *canê*, I hear you've fallen in love. If the girl is prettier than I am, then congratulations to you. But if she is uglier, then may all the woes of Baghdad rain upon your head. The husband does not answer. Alan sang quietly at first, but with growing energy. By the third cigarette and seventeenth stanza, when the wife finally sees for herself that her husband's new wife is ugly as a slop pail, Alan felt cheerful enough to venture out of bed. He tried the shower and found it adequate. It had been two weeks since his last manicure and pedicure, and he grumbled about the state of his hands. He hadn't shaved in three days, when he had hastily removed his dagger-shaped *simbêlpîj* moustache for his sentencing, because it was such a trademark. He had left his sideburns, though. Now he was free but he had plenty of misery to complain about: his trousers were stiff, and he had no clean change of underwear. He enjoyed his breakfast of bread and butter, another cigarette, his mood improving. He finished the milk, pulled on his coat and hurried outside.

The sun was beaming a giant spotlight on women crowding the street. But his interest waned. Most of them were very old, or in the company of small children or large shopping bags. And squinting in bright light gave one wrinkles. Alan remembered his sunglasses, lying on the foyer table in Istanbul. He had needed two full working days to pick out that pair. He crossed the street, entered the garage. The elevator door stood open in welcome, but he skirted it, cavorting down the steps. Number 45. Hello there, my special friend, my own taxi. It had a docile look, an old but reliable vehicle. In Istanbul, he would have refused a lift in it. Nor did the car seem impressed by him. The doors resisted speedy opening; they needed to be coaxed, nicely. Finally they allowed him inside. He placed his cigarettes on the seat, and began his inspection: first the exterior, the nooks and crannies beneath, and then the frayed interior. He pulled away foot rugs, ashtrays, prised off the mirror, and ran his hands under the seats. No electronic devices.

He had a look at himself in the rear-view mirror. It was too dark in the garage to see the details, but even so, he admired his face with stubble on it. He opened his lips a crack; his white teeth gleamed. A bit like one of the singers at the

Gazino, who cultivated a three-day beard to show that they didn't care about their appearance. But the shadow on his cheeks gave his face more of a fragile look, he thought, and wondered whether he wasn't beginning to resemble Mem Alan, the Kurdish monarch . . . except that Mem Alan had died as a teenager, all for the love of Zin. Alan had never liked that saga. He felt ashamed of his people, taking as their national heroes a couple that had died young, for love! No wonder the thirty million Kurds couldn't manage to put together a country of their own.

He flashed himself a goodbye smile in the mirror, and got back to work. He found another map of New York City in one of the door pouches. He slid behind the wheel, and spread the map on the seat next to him. Someone had thoughtfully placed two x's in red, and pencilled the route between them. One x represented his apartment. The other was Erkal's house. He backed the car carefully out of its haven.

He began his first full day in America with a little bit of small talk.

Car Attendant: Hey, how ya doin.

Alan: Hello. Fine, thank you.

He found his way back to Broadway easily, and headed due south, downtown. He had the nerves of a prophet and the pushing and shoving of New York City traffic did not trouble him in the least. In Istanbul, the cars were smaller, but nastier. He passed a large building complex, with a crowd of people lining the kerb in front. Their faces turned towards his taxi, their expressions, like donkeys at feeding

27

time, eager, competitive. But there were strange breeds among them, mixing casually, including Orientals with misshapen eyes, and many *yam-yam*. As his car approached, a pale man jumped off the kerb and began running towards the cab, waving his arm. Alan swerved adroitly, but had to stop at a red light. The panting man reached Alan's car. When he put his hand on the door handle, Alan stepped hard on the gas pedal. The man's hand flicked away. Alan watched his face in the rear-view mirror, saw the baby skin turning as red as the traffic light he was just flaunting. The man shook his fist.

Nothing in life had prepared Alan for this. Sweat did not douse but fuelled the rage that had broken out in him. His face and shirt were drenched instantly. He hated sweating, for cosmetic reasons. And he did not have a change of shirt. He aimed his vehicle at the middle of the road, where he felt protected by the traffic from the clamouring populace. Broadway is hilly up in that part of town, and picturesque, the way Beyoglu is, his neighbourhood of Istanbul, with people milling about, and shops selling their wares on the street. He caught glimpses of women as he drove by – they didn't look shy. Many were plump, the way Alan liked them, and brightly dressed. But if you just keep going downriver for several more miles, the neighbourhood changes, and begins to match the pictures Alan knew from movies, or from postcards the butcher in his village had taped to his wall, bragging that he had a friend there – the buildings scrape the sky. That is, they appear to move, the clouds whizzing along increase their momentum – they threaten to fall. In short, Alan felt trapped and he kept his eyes low, on distractions, and noted that many of the women were much too thin, but they didn't look dull-eyed with hunger either. Their eyes looked horribly alert. They would be reluctant to give themselves to him, Alan guessed. They preferred clasping their handbags. In Istanbul, where his name was familiar to all, a kind of national poem, the girls were honoured to be of service. He was nearing his destination, when he fell into the clutches of another traffic light.

Is not freedom of movement God-given? How can any self-respecting democracy meddle in man's natural right to move any way he pleases? In Istanbul, where driving is a competitive sport, each man for himself, traffic lights are a symbol of authority's smashed hopes. If the light is green, a driver might be in the mood to take his time, while waiting at a red light will get you nudged violently from behind by someone in a hurry. The pedestrians are canny dodgers. Only strangers get killed, crossing at the green. But in New York they might manage their affairs differently. Alan didn't want to be noticed for the wrong reasons, and heeded the red light. As so often happens, obedience was punished. An intruder leaped inside his car, swinging a sharp-edged black briefcase. Alan could not get rid of him again; remember, he was still unarmed. The passenger with the nerve wore cashmere despite the adolescent pimples on his chin, and the tone of his conversation was imperative. Alan understood nothing besides the explanation points.

'*Galegale! Galegale!! Fez!!!*'

Alan shook his head. When the light turned green, he drove to the opposite kerb and halted there.

The passenger's tone changed.

'Qijevij??! Galegale!! Qijevij??!!!'

Alan lit a cigarette and puffed patiently, watching the passenger in the rear-view mirror. Between puffs, he sang a little in Kurdish to calm his nerves, the song of the rich virgin who fell in love with a poor shepherd, but the poor shepherd was not interested.

His demeanour frightened the passenger. He jumped out of the taxi as if the seat was burning. Somehow, he simultaneously pulled out a Dictaphone, and peered at the licence plates, babbled something into the microphone. Alan turned and stretched to lock both back doors. He drove away at a leisure tempo. But he hadn't travelled more than a few yards when another man grabbed at his car. From all sides, people were running towards the cab. They grabbed the door handle, and when they couldn't open it, they shouted or banged on the roof. In the meantime, traffic had thickened, slowed, came to a halt. Fate ordered a rest. If all those strangers hadn't been paying attention to Alan, he would have enjoyed it.

Traffic is probably to blame for the lamentable attitude that city dwellers have towards time. The New Yorker, for instance, considers standstill a form of extreme pain, while you and I know that there is nothing as comfortable, nothing as existentially life-affirming as a moment, or preferably many moments of complete standstill. When faced with time, a New Yorker either 'takes advantage' of it or he 'kills' it, whereas a Kurd 'accompanies' it. He does not despise tedium. He welcomes it, as the venerable father of his best ideas. So it occurred to Alan to roll down the windows of his taxi, and allow the cold air to take a seat. The vehicle cooled down quickly. And no one wanted to share a taxi with so much cold air. Pedestrians no longer attempted to climb in unasked, he was no longer mobbed by the *falan-filan*. Still, they did look up when he drove by, they did approach him, wearing fervently hopeful expressions. But then they stopped, and turned away. Soon, Alan reached the subject's house, where he was in for another shock.

*   *   *

The subject's house lay on a small side street. You don't want to lose your way on the side street of a wealthy neighbourhood in Manhattan. It's like getting lost in a cemetery. No one speaks. All you see is stone, and names on stone, and any living people walking about look preoccupied and sad. Alan intended to park his car, and sit in the car for a while, watching the subject's house. The street offered plenty of free parking spaces; he found a place directly in front of the address. He relaxed, smoking and watching the dour brown building that stood protected by high iron gates and the rubbery shrubs that only grow in New York concrete. A flight of steep stairs had to be negotiated to the front door. The sidewalk was quiet except for a neon tracksuit and waterproof sneakers that darted by a dozen times at regular intervals, always at the same clip. Much later, the front door opened, and a stout woman in a maid's uniform appeared.

As she was monitoring the street, two children pushed by

her, tripping down the steps to the garden. She scolded them shrilly from above. They paid no attention. She continued her tirade as the two girls calmly unloaded two white mice from their pockets on to the garden walk.

Through the open windows of his taxi, Alan heard what he had suspected – she shrieked in Turkish. The girls had snapped leashes on the mice, and were strolling with them. The creatures wore tiny blue sweaters. The children wore jackets so thick they could hardly move their arms. After glancing up at the front door and establishing that they had broken the maid's will, beaten her into a full retreat, they hastily removed their coats, shaking them off on to the ground. Their blue uniforms hung askew, their knee socks swaddled their ankles, their long black braids were coming unravelled. They had wild black eyes, with long thick lashes. They knelt on the icy ground and played nose to nose with the mice.

After a while, a spry red sports car pulled up alongside Alan's taxi and stopped. So did his heart, as he watched a really splendid-looking woman step out of the front seat. She wore a lovely outfit, with a short Persian-lamb skirt and a jacket to match, and high heels in the snow. As astonishing as someone walking on water: black patent-leather heels walking on snow. Even the icy sidewalk could not defeat them. She kept her head high, her gleaming black hair bobbed at her shoulders, earrings sparkled beneath her ears, her cheeks were flushed, her eyes looking at nothing in particular, she did not exercise caution, but steered towards the children, her legs glistening in nylon stockings. They spotted her, gathered up their mice, wrapped their little hands around the bars of the gate, pushed their faces between them and called, 'Mommy! Mommy!'

She beamed, threw open the gate and swept both children up in her arms. She lugged them up the flight of stairs like that, her stilettos punching through the snow to click on the stone. When she reached the landing, she turned around and looked down at the street, at the car she had just left. It was idling a few yards ahead. Her face became sombre. Her black eyes fixed on the red car, as it picked up speed. She had the same long black lashes as her daughters. Only when the car had turned a corner did she open the front door, and proceed inside.

Alan felt relief. The children were very pleasant. Their mother was pleasant. Alan hated working with people he didn't like. He was all for pleasantness and politeness. He kept repeating her name, 'Mommy'. He thought it was one of the prettiest names for a woman he had ever heard.

*   *   *

No sooner had these warm thoughts eddied through the cold regions of his plans, than a uniformed torso appeared in his window. He saw the Colt in a cheap holster, the blue trouser leg.

He said, 'Hello, sir.'

He was forced to correct himself, 'Hello, madam.'

Alan had known many women in his life. He had never felt uneasy with them, because he felt he could, with some on-the-spot adjusting of his facial expressions or tone of voice, control them. He had never needed to resort to violence. He had known modest salesgirls, powerful mothers, spoiled actresses, known them all. But he had never met an armed woman. Another *yam-yam*.

The policewoman had other concerns. She had not yet issued her quota of tickets, and her meeting with Alan had the graciousness of a pounce. There is no reason to remember how she addressed him – it is too terrible. All '*Galegale*' and communicating total indifference to his looks. Her English was not worth much either – it had the cadence of impatience and impudence common to big cities. We don't hear that sort of thing here, and I hope you never will. He understood only '*Mista*'. He even caught himself taking an interest in the odd local syllables as she chanted '*kamonkamonkamon*' and then he saw her brown fist descend on to the yellow hood of the car, and he heard the drum beat.

When he stepped out of the cab, he was planning to teach her civility, without the use of language. But then he realized by the smile that cracked open on her face that he was following orders, doing precisely what she had told him to do. Before he could raise his hand against her, her own little hand on the large gun on her hip, her robust stature and also the fact that she was of a strange race dissuaded him. Meanwhile, he understood from certain gestures she was making that she wanted to see his car papers. Mr Ballinger had put them in the glove compartment. It transpired that all his documents were in order, but she felt a certain shortcoming in them, and she wanted to add a few more: she handed him a yellow piece of paper. It matched the colour of

34

his car. He took it, and because nothing else occurred to him, he said 'Thank you'. This apparently surprised her no end. She peered at him closely, before shaking her head in disgust. Finally, she walked away without seeming to care whether he followed her orders or not. She wore a short jacket that called attention to her gun but also to her *qun* – her trousers were filled to capacity. He wondered whether she had put on extra underpants, to increase the volume. He had always suspected the women in his village wore extra skirts for that reason.

When she was out of sight, he nosed his cab out of the parking space, and drove around the block. He encountered a red light at every corner, and during this interval, he was so confused he could neither swallow nor spit. He mumbled what he knew of English: 'Hello goodbye donut thankyou Hollywood.' He tried to concentrate on his driving. But he couldn't stop grumbling about the natives: he was noticing their habit of double-parking their vehicles, while leaving the opposite kerb entirely empty. On narrow streets, like the one where the Erkals lived, perfectly good spaces were left vacant. There could be no reasonable explanation for this. He scorned the New Yorkers for being peculiar. He spotted a garage but a man sitting in a booth at the entrance waved his hands at him, shooing him backwards, pointing at a sign that he could not read. He understood that he was being rejected. He reversed his car, and circled the block, again and again. Time accompanied him and soothed him. After a while, he pulled into the same parking space from which he had been banished, and waited. He was hoping that Mommy would come out again. He hoped she would not change her shoes.

The most important part of an assassin's job is waiting, and the most important talent he has is patience. He must never rush things. He has to relax. That is why assassins generally have such a long life-expectancy. Because they have learned to take their time. Alan sat in his cab, marking the passing seconds with his heartbeat, the minutes not at all, and each hour with a cigarette. He became hungry and thirsty. He thought about eating *çiĝköfte*, a dish he had never touched in Istanbul. He had considered it primitive, a country meal that men made – they rolled raw chopped meat in their hands till it was like clay. Then, in front of everyone, in a grand celebratory way, they tested its consistency by forming a ball, and hurling this at the ceiling. If it stuck there, then the meat was ready to be eaten. *Hila hila, çiĝköfte*. He had despised it in Istanbul, and now his mouth watered at the thought.

Dusk set in gradually, the street lamps turned on, and then a limousine pulled up in front of the house. A white sealskin coat got out of the back door, a uniform out of the other. The uniform produced an umbrella, and led the fur coat to the house.

The owner of the fur coat was muffled by a red scarf and topped by a felt hat. Briefly, he turned his head towards Alan, eyeing the taxi. Alan looked into his face, and lost control over his heart. It began a wild dance of horror. Since his boyhood, he had known this face, feared it, hated it, and nourished the fantasy that he, he alone, would someday cut off its ears, and carry them as a trophy. In an interview, Sulymon Erkal had referred to his ears as 'Gandhi ears', although he had little in common with Mr Gandhi. In the years since his retirement from the military, his face had not appeared in the papers, but rumours had kept it familiar. One heard that Sulymon had led a healthy Kurdish prisoner to a coffin, forced him inside, and then invited his family to attend the funeral. The prisoner's mother had been upset about not being allowed to wash the body beforehand. Loud solemn music was played at the burial, which drowned out the buried man's screams, but most audible of all was Sulymon Erkal's conversation about the stock market. Alan remembered this and at once, the rage set in. He would have jumped out of the car and attacked those earlobes and everything else that came with them. But then his phone rang.

Mr Ballinger calling.

'Beautiful day.'

'Yes.'

'Where are you?'

'At the house.'

'Everything OK?'

'Of course.'

'You're not very talkative.'

'When are you giving me the weapon?'

'Not today. Tomorrow. So tell me, how do you like driving a taxi? Did you figure out the traffic rules?'

'Goodbye, then.'

By the time Alan looked up, the fur-coated man had reached the house, and the chauffeur was standing outside getting wet to hold the front door open for him. After the door swept shut, the uniformed chauffeur hurried back to the car, and made his own escape.

*　　*　　*

Alan had been without a weapon since his arrest a week ago, and the absence of this creature comfort made him feel incomplete, as if he had suddenly lost the use of a limb. He was too experienced to believe his karate skills could ever get him out a real jam. And another thing: Alan was a diva who was used to having unpleasant chores connected with his work taken care of by someone else. He had never worked without an assistant. In Istanbul, he had enjoyed a series of female assistants who toiled for him in exchange for his affections – they would take his car to the garage for oil changes, type any bureaucratic correspondence, buy him gun magazines. Once, it had even been necessary for him to promise marriage to a woman to keep her in his employ. But this had proved an unsatisfactory arrangement because no sooner did the words come out of his mouth in a fit of giddiness, when she refused his advances, than she was yielding to his advances, in fact she was demanding them all the time, but refusing to take care of his chores and expected instead that he take care of hers. It took him no time at all to replace her. In fact, he replaced her several times over. So his helplessness in the New World was manifold, and overrode any curiosity he might have felt about the place. His hosts had not even equipped with him with the cosmetics necessary to make himself presentable to a woman, supplying neither a change of clothing, nor a toothbrush.

Alan found enough money in the wallet to go on a shopping spree. He had noticed a small store in his neighbourhood; he shopped without paying attention to the prices – he was not at all interested in money, so in practice he was neither parsimonious nor spendthrift. He loaded his cart with cola, cartons which he hoped contained milk, white bread, cigarettes (sadly, they did not carry his beloved Samsuns), jam, toothbrush, shaving equipment, underwear in plastic packs (any small Turkish store offered an equal range of products) and . . . and . . . he kept adding to the cart. By the time he reached the checkout counter, and unpacked, he was drawing attention to himself with the quantity of his supplies – why didn't he go one block down to the big supermarket, if he was doing a major shopping? – and the contents, including a pair of dusty black-framed sunglasses he had discovered at the back of the store, a vial of cheap perfume, a woman's pocket mirror and a huge pack of *preservatifi*.

The elderly cashier did not bat an eyelash.

Alan tried to jar her by remarking enthusiastically, 'America!' by which he meant, 'What extraordinarily large packs of *preservatifi* you sell here!'

But she only glared at him with the hostility of a low-level bureaucrat, while she packed his groceries, sighing and dropping them with studied slowness into a paper bag.

He had made the last purchase with vague hopes that he might be in need of such a thing. He didn't want to be caught empty-handed. He did not know much about illness, but had a horror of making a girl carry a load, and having to pay for it with a marriage certificate. Middle Eastern families were adamant in this respect. His thoughts turned often to Mommy, nor had he forgotten the policewoman, or Pat, the donut girl. He was not a fan of abstinence, but he was too proud to buy himself a woman.

He passed the donut shop on his way home, and went in, his head held high, his gait purposeful. Pat was refilling the display case with donuts, picking them up delicately with tongs. He strolled up to the counter, and waited for her attention. Finally, she came to him.

He said, 'Coffee, please,' his gaze ramming into her brown eyes.

She became short of breath. Her oranges quivered, as if a truck was passing by a market stall. The *Kir* saluted them. She turned around to pour him coffee and he saw the generous expanse back there, a field that would seat seven tribes. She caught his look as she turned around, and her mood softened even more. As she placed the Styrofoam coffee cup in front of him, she laid her donut of a hand on his. He brought it to his lips. He kissed the dark plump knuckles. His *Kir* nearly poked a hole into the counter.

Unfortunately, when Alan entered the donut shop, Pat was nowhere to be seen, and a young man stood at the counter in her place, ruining Alan's appetite. He back-tracked. His arms ached; he felt humiliated to be carrying his own groceries. All of his complaints gathered and started a terrible squawking in his brain, so that he stopped heeding

40

his intuition, and as a consequence he had no idea that he was heading home to yet another and even more serious compromise of his lifestyle.

*   *   *

He reached his building, that evening of his second night in the New World, and recognized someone. In the foyer, a figure mopped the floor with savage energy. He struck him as familiar, and indeed, it proved to be the Driver. But now he was wearing a janitor's orange suit. Alan walked right up to him and stared. The Driver straightened up slowly, as though he was suddenly very tired. He decided to make conversation. You want to know what he said, even though Alan could not understand a word of it? Sure. Although I hope you don't understand it too well, either.

He said, 'This sure is a mother *faki* job. Ballinger wants me to help him out with you. He kept me after his company bought this house. On the condition I take care of a few extras. I says, what extras. He says, oh just driving me around from time to time, nothing more. Then next thing I knows he's expecting me to keep an eye on the tenants. Wonder what he'll want tomorrow. And he ain't paying me shit. So I'm not doin' it. I'm just minding my own business. You need something in the ways of janitorial help, call me. I ain't bothering you otherwise. I live down in the basement. With my kids. And the rats. My wife was smart, she left.' He laughed.

Something in Alan's stance – he wasn't budging, and he did have a reputation – unnerved the janitor.

He looked around for help and called, 'Oh, there's Mrs Allen!'

The name confused our hero, breaking his concentration. He heard the front door open behind him, and turned around. An old woman was entering the lobby, dressed in gleaming white sneakers, a very worn pink coat, and a floral knitted hat that resembled a tea cosy. She moved towards the stairwell, and then stopped, staring at the janitor. Her eyes, two blue slits in an old but taut face, had a peculiar shine to them, and her cheeks glistened. She was crying.

'Hello,' she stammered. Then she turned back to the stairs.

Alan had tired of the conversation and, after giving the janitor one last hostile stare, he turned his back towards him with studied carelessness and followed Mrs Allen to the staircase. He would have overtaken her on the first landing, would have continued his quick ascent, but as he was passing, she put her gnarled hand on his elbow from behind and held on to him, remarking, 'Thank you so much.' He was forced to take the stairs slowly, one step at a time, and with frequent intermissions, clutching his shopping bags with his shooting hand. His hand began to feel sore, and he worried about injuring it. She required six flights of assistance, as she lived on the same floor as he did. Now he remembered Mr Ballinger's warning about the neighbour. So this was the Allen who lived behind the neighbouring door, which he had to unlock for her. And of course she succeeded in inviting him inside. There was no mistaking her intention: she held on to his elbow and kept going over the threshold. Now, this was against his principles. But she succeeded in manoeuvring him there, into her lair. It had been years since he had set foot inside someone else's house. Even his girlfriends in Istanbul came to him, or he paid for a hotel.

Her apartment astonished him. The first room looked like a library, with two tables, one against the wall and covered with books, the other in the middle of the room, on which a typewriter jutted out from under a pile of papers. The white cabinets that lined the walls were also stuffed with books. She let go of his arm, and pushed the typewriter aside, shovelled the papers together with her small crooked hands, speaking all the time. Then she removed books off the other table, and revealed a stove. He saw the refrigerator in the corner, the sink. He was too amazed to leave, his legs grew roots.

Finally she stopped speaking, looked him over, and asked, 'Turkish?'

He was stung and replied, 'No, no.' And then he added, in Kurdish, '*Ez Ingilizi nuezanum.*'

To his astonishment, she repeated this phrase in Kurdish, as if she was savouring it, and then translated it: 'I don't speak English.' She seemed pleased. 'I invite you for dinner,' she said in Turkish. She added, 'I can't speak Kurmanci, because I never had a reason to learn it. We'll have to meet on phonetically strange ground. Put your bags down and take a seat. I am having an absolutely bad mood. My bridge party has been cancelled. It is a calamity for me, really.'

Alan was an inexperienced fool. He thought it perfectly natural that a New Yorker should recognize not only his mother tongue, but also the particular dialect. He was not about to reward her with conversation.

43

'Yes, thank you,' he grunted, ashamed about his lack of interest in her; she was an old, respectable woman.

When Mrs Allen hung her pink coat over one chair he gave in, hanging his coat over the other chair, and putting his packages down on the floor. She placed a teapot on the table, and dropped her floral knitted hat on top; a perfect fit. She set the table with some dark bread, two tins of sardines, and two tomatoes. Her attempts at opening the sardines prompted her guest to help. The sardine tin is an instrument of torture that should be reported to Amnesty International – it lures the hungry into opening it, and spatters him in the process with fishy-smelling oil. And you know how Alan hated stains. He took a rag from her sink, and vigorously rubbed the spots in his shirt and trousers; to no avail. This was not a minor matter, but a metaphysical insult. The sardines smelled good though, calming his nerves.

'You must eat. Sardines will lower your cholesterol. And they're cheap. What a miserable condition I am in. Miserable. My bridge partners are moving to Florida. Playing bridge has been my only form of a social life. I have no one else. I will never see my son again. That's my own fault. All because I am an atheist. As any sensible person is. As any person with a little bit of brains in his head has to be.' And then she regarded him and remarked, 'I am boring you into a coma.'

He lit a cigarette and she did not protest. She gave him a gold-rimmed teacup to use as an ashtray.

When he had finished the cigarette she pointed to the food and said, 'Good appetite.'

Natural good manners had prevented him from simply saying, No, no, and creeping away – a Kurd respects hospitality – but good manners would not permit him to eat, either, until the host had begged him over and over, and with increasing hysteria, to give him the inestimable pleasure of sharing his food.

When the old woman cried, 'Please do eat,' for the fifth time, he relented.

He did not pay attention to her monologue over dinner, so there is no point in repeating it.

After an interval he deemed polite, he stood up, and said, 'Thank you.' He would not say more. He did not wish to speak to her.

She had rings around her pale-blue eyes that seemed to mark the decades, and a small turned-up nose that must have been pretty a half-century earlier.

'I have to thank you,' she said. She remained seated. 'You're good company. You are as old as my son. I had him at thirty-five. That was old for my generation but I didn't want a husband. I got married, you know, because I was bedazzled by sex. At that time, you couldn't sleep with a man, like now. That was not done. Not in our circle. I was a very beautiful woman. I was aware of it. That is why I couldn't write my doctoral thesis. I was too absent-minded, distracted by this sex. So I got married, and then I finally wrote my thesis and got my doctorate, my thesis – never mind, it's all about books, I don't want to bore you to extinction – and then I got pregnant, and I had a very nice son. Who I will never see again.'

She said this without much pathos. His grandmother had probably wailed for three months when he left home for Istanbul. He backed out of the kitchen, remembering to take his shopping bags. Her curly hair was white and looked fluffy.

She waved from the table, 'Close the door behind you, please.'

As he was pulling the door shut, he heard her sigh.

He passed his second evening in America scrubbing the sardine stains from his trousers, trying to recognize individual cockroaches – he couldn't – and smoking. He had the habit of lighting his matches on his palm, or on his elbow, or another hard body part, when he had the privacy to expose that. Although this last feat would surely have aroused admiration in others, he had never performed it in front of a public. The truth is, he was nearly always hard where many men were nearly always soft. But on this particular evening, Alan was too tired to show off to himself. He was even too tired to shave, although he had been looking forward to that. But he needed strength to decide what kind of moustache he was going to grow. He was aware of eighteen alternatives. He felt it was time to switch from the knife-like *simbêlpîj* to something grander, like the *simbêlpalik*, which swept over most of one's face. The sideburns could go.

After he had finished another pack of cigarettes, he decided to draw up a list of things he missed from home. His lawyer in Istanbul had lent him a pen, which he had squirrelled away, as this wasn't the sort of object he would ever buy. Now he congratulated himself on this forethought, took the pen from his jacket pocket, and opened his English book, writing on the back cover:

Kekikli Pirsola
Schoebyat

They were his favourite dishes. Then he added:

View of the Bosphorus from the tenth floor
Made-to-order snakeskin shoes,
Television while falling asleep
Stereo music while entertaining girls – recordings of
Feqyê Teyra
Red velvet curtains.
Twinkling burglar-alarm system
The wet bar (a whisky!)
My nice big bed (fits three girls)
Custom-made jeep
Samsuns

He placed the pen back in his jacket, and stretched out on his cot. He was worried about the weapon – Mr Ballinger had not called back, and he had no idea when he was going to be able to finish his job. He tossed and turned. That strange Western wailing came through the walls again. *'Traurigkeit,'* sang a woman. He muttered 'OK,' and opened his English dictionary to the T's. He felt proud to be so studious, opening a book for the second time that evening. He found the word trout. Must be a folk song. A light snowfall came through the open window.

Alan imagined himself entering his favourite club in Beyoglu, where the prominent politicians and wealthier businessmen met, ordering lentil soup with lemon, and his friends surrounding him, pounding him on the back, welcoming him back from his vacation. Women had a way of circling around him with their gazes. By gazing back, he snared them. He had money in his pocket, as much as he wanted. Someone anticipated his smallest wish – did he want a drink? It was on its way to him. The more money one had, the less one seemed to pay for things; wealth seemed to engender new wealth. He had been rich by the time he was twenty years old. He took his wealth and his success completely for granted. The arrest had not surprised him particularly – it was just a change in the direction fate was taking, which would affect his lifestyle for a while, but never his position in society. Before he could study its new direction, fate veered again. He was now in the middle of this veering motion: fate had not yet come to a stop. For the time being, he fell asleep.

THREE

THE THIRD DAY BEGAN with a bath, and afterwards an anointment with perfume. Finally, he shaved, taking off the sideburns, and leaving the contours of a bushy *simbêl-palik*. After getting dressed, he had a final look at himself in his new pocket mirror, and then he returned to the bathroom and shaved a little more, having rejected the lavish moustache on the grounds that it might draw attention. He decided on the more modest *simbêltûj*. It took some doing, making sure to create enough, but not too much, of a space in the middle. Tapering the ends required a delicate touch with the shaver.

Soon afterwards, having fortified himself with coffee and donuts from the donut store – still no sign of Pat, who clearly worked the night shift – he headed out in his taxi. He was feeling rested and competent. He had some planning to do. First, he would have to deal with the possibility that Mr Ballinger did not intend to give him a gun – perhaps guns were so common that they had grown out of fashion in

America – and so the fashion-conscious Mr Ballinger expected him to do the job with a sharp instrument instead. Surely, he would have his reasons. Alan was not a novice to this method, but he disliked it, because it was much more intimate, the tearing sounds bothered him, and the mess was harder to control.

Meanwhile, the forces of nature were preparing to attack the city. The city resisted, putting up a front of stony indifference. People were scurrying for cover, or, their faces desperate and pinched, they were flagging taxis in a manner more piteous than demanding. Suddenly, the other taxis followed Alan's example – they, too, ignored these pathetic pedestrians, and drove past them slowly, keeping their doors locked. Inside, one could see the drivers with smug expressions enjoying the warmth, their radios. They drove intently, to their 'home', Alan figured. Traffic was light, the streets amusingly slippery. Alan reached his destination quickly, pulled into his accustomed parking space directly in front of the door, and let the motor idle. He turned on the radio. A man was expounding, enunciating each word, perfect for a learner. Alan made a sincere effort. 'All experience has shown that mankind . . .'

'Hekspir . . .' Alan tried.

'. . . are more disposed to suffer, where evils are sufferable.'

'Sufa . . . sufad,' said Alan.

How easy English was! He concentrated and did not see the danger: the front door of the subject's house opened and shut. Mommy and the maid took him by complete surprise, climbing into the car from two sides, slamming the doors,

50

and before he could defend himself he heard a sharp voice ordering him, 'Let's go!'

One of them had spoken, either the dowdy Turkish maid in lumpy boots, or, more likely, Mommy, elegant in a long lambskin coat and red pocketbook that she held on her lap. One of these two had ordered him to drive them! As if he was their employee. As if he was a common *kapüçe*, the servant in the expensive apartment buildings, to be bossed around by young and old. As if he was a taxi driver, and not Alan, a name that made certain quarters of Istanbul tremble.

Mommy babbled at him in English, and flagged her hand, indicating straight ahead. She followed this with a vigorous winding motion, commanding him to roll up the windows. And he knew: I must do what I am told.

'It's freezing in here,' said Mommy to her companion in Turkish. 'He must be going through the changes!' They laughed loudly, assuming he could not understand them.

Although they addressed each other with strict recognition of their social differences – the first name, Tuerkan, for the maid, and the title, Ajda Hanim, for her employer – they spoke with the ease of trusting intimates, gleeful about their luck at finding a taxi directly in front of the house during a snowstorm. And then the cabby had proven kind enough to take them, when he clearly had something better to do, given the weather. In the Orient, showing generosity is a moral requirement, but in New York, generosity suggests you are a dupe. His passengers had lived long enough in the New World to appreciate that the taxi driver, having good character, was weak, a pushover.

'Let's swing by the shop secretly and spy on my husband. If he's still working, I can visit my girlfriend. Driver! You'll pass Fifth Avenue and Tenth Street and stop there, before going again.'

'And if he's not, Ajda Hanim?'

'Then we'll have to hurry. Because I would really like to pay a short visit to my friend. My husband should be there. He had a two-million-dollar sale scheduled for tomorrow and I won't allow it. Sale's off. He's having an unpleasant meeting with the angry client later today.'

'Rugs again, Ajda Hanim?'

'Yes, of course, for two million!' They laughed for several blocks about this. After which his wife said, 'That buyer only pays in counterfeit money. It's absolutely safe, he says, come straight from a government agency. I can't tell the difference myself. But I'm not having it. I want proper money in my wallet.'

'Really! Fake money!' gushed the maid. 'How exciting. I've never seen any.'

'Yes you have, Tuerkan,' her companion replied drily. 'Anyway, my husband plans to call off the deal. I don't need any money, actually. I need American citizenship and a lawyer.'

'Why do you need a lawyer, Ajda Hanim? Can't you share your husband's? Cohn Mister. A smart, hard-working man. There's Sulymon Bey. He's alone. Working. He's such a hard worker,' the maid praised him. 'Not like my husband.'

And then Ajda Erkal called in English, 'Keep driving straight ahead.'

Alan craned his neck to catch a glimpse of Sulymon, and nearly drove into a double-parked truck.

His passengers gasped with pleasurable fear, as if they were on a roller-coaster ride, and giggled, 'Two babes in the back, and his steering wheel gets too stiff to turn!'

Alan concentrated on the road.

'Tuerkan, I am having a change of plans. Why am I bothering to come along now? You can easily pick up both of our passport photos. That way I can stay in this taxi, and we'll go to the agency together another time, when the weather's better. You can give me my photos tomorrow. But make sure the pictures are pretty before you pay for them. Oh, what does it matter! They'll be fine. And don't forget not to tell anyone of our little plan. Especially not your husband. You surprise him one day with your pretty blue passport.'

'Ajda Hanim, the taxi driver is driving in the wrong direction!'

'Mister! Turn here! (He's dimwitted, Tuerkan.)'

'There, now he understands.'

'Now hop out, and I'll see you tomorrow! Driver, continue to Greene Street, corner of Prince.'

Ajda Erkal leaned back in the seat with a sign of relief. But then she noticed the driver's nameplate. She sat up very straight, and he could feel her breath on the back of his head.

After a while she said, 'Alan Korkunc . . . are you Turkish?'

She tried to inspect him more closely, and noticed that the meter was not turned on and he could charge her whatever he chose.

Whereupon she snapped in Turkish, 'Is your meter broken?' And then realizing that her incredible luck – the last taxi happened to have been in front of the door – was about to turn incredibly sour, she added in an assuaging voice, 'Are you Turkish, brother?'

When he didn't reply, she asked again, 'Alan Bey, are you Turkish?'

This time Alan replied in English, 'Yes.'

She sat back in the seats, and he watched a scowl settle over her lovely features.

'Do you know how to get to Prince and Greene?'

'No, madam,' he said.

She directed him, the corners of her mouth twitching, as if she was about to cry. When they reached the street, she stepped out of the cab and came to the window. He rolled it down.

She handed him a hundred-dollar bill and said in a matter-of-fact way, as if she was ordering groceries, 'I know your name and your cab number. You mind your own business. Because otherwise . . .'

He looked briefly into the glaring headlights of her eyes, pretended to find them blinding, and looked down again. She walked off, reassured, a spoiled and determined Turkish Zin. He found her attempts to threaten him adorable: so feminine.

At that moment, Alan's phone rang.

'Where the hell are you going?' asked Mr Ballinger. 'Taking a tour?'

Alan replied, 'I'm working. I'll call you back.'

Ajda Erkal was strolling briskly, as if the matter was forgotten, and he drove away. He regretted that he had spoken to her at all. He did not want to have any kind of intercourse with his victims, he must come out of the blue, he must not have a voice.

When he finally returned to his garage, he investigated the taxi with the energy of the enraged, trying to figure out where the bug was planted. Mr Ballinger was obviously following him. And taking pleasure in his problems. The bug must be found. He tore into the seats, yanked out the radio, the light bulbs. He broke two fingernails, *zu zu*! he must have a manicure. But his imperative had no force, he found nothing. When he had the opportunity, he would paint Mr Ballinger's fate black. It would be a rare pleasure. Would would would.

*   *   *

He reached the red-brick house, the dark lobby. The sounds and odours of food baking and frying flooded the stairwell. The old woman was ahead of him on the stairs, dragging packages. Alan hung back. But then he heard her stumble, and cry out. He ran. She was still upright, leaning against the metal railing, trying to balance herself. A paper shopping bag was slipping from her hands. He grabbed it. She watched him, shaking her head with relief. He offered his spare elbow to her. She accepted, she held on. But he was appalled.

He hadn't come to America to help people carry their packages home. And then get invited inside. And prove himself unable to refuse.

'Will you have a drink?' she asked him in Turkish, as they crossed the threshold.

Actually, he felt quite glad to see the kitchen again, because at least he recognized it, and familiarity had become more attractive to him. She had obviously tidied up. Her papers stood in orderly heaps. There was room for the bags of groceries on the table, and without aforethought, he unpacked and put everything away in the refrigerator. He had never done this himself. He did scorn her refrigerator; it didn't even have an ice-maker. She was leafing through her papers, while he tidied up for her.

'I am writing a little story,' she said. 'It is about a child who finds a newt in a pond, and names him God. God lives in a glass jar in the child's room. The child loves him very much. But you can imagine how he gets into trouble. Of course it will never be published. In the land of the free, no reputable magazine will publish a story that smacks of blasphemy. I assume you're not a religious believer.'

Alan was embarrassed. Most of the killers that he knew believed. They prayed and had regular contact with Allah. The only time anything of that sort crossed his mind was when he received new proof that he was not immune to ageing. Allah occurred to him, as a kind of reference, like a quote one heard all the time, when he spotted a new white hair on his head, or on his chest. Then he pulled the hair out. He didn't bow to anyone, why to a higher force? If there was such a thing, he didn't want to know about it. But he didn't feel like talking about it, so he said nothing.

'Oh well, never mind. I will reward you for your help.

Please take a seat.' She was sure he would accept. 'You must have some of my husband's sherry. My husband would have wanted that. He would have said, "Two gentlemen caught in a snowstorm must drink sherry," if he had been the one caught in the storm, and not me. But I was caught because he is dead.'

Alan was too astonished by her lack of sentimentality to protest, so she poured him a large glass, and without hesitating, she poured herself one too. Now Alan took off his coat, hung it on back of the chair, and sat down.

She cried, 'Oh my gosh, I am still wearing my coat too!' and followed suit.

'And now: drink!' she said. Alan tasted the sherry; she did too. She was clearly waiting for him to say something, and although it was very much against his principles to speak for no reason, his good manners prevailed and he said, 'Very good.'

She laughed with pleasure and amended, 'Very good and very cheap. Only $5 a bottle.' She raised her glass and pronounced, *'Prosit!'*

So he raised his and said, *'Noş.'*

'Yes, of course, *noş*,' she said.

She went on, 'That's the best part about America, that the essentials in life are cheap. This coat cost only $9.99. I bought it when we got here, in 1950. It was second-hand. It is a spring coat, actually. In winter, I wear a bathrobe inside it. It's the only coat I ever had in this country. But I don't want another. I would pay someone a salary to keep possessions away from me.'

This took Alan aback. He was fond of possessions. In Istanbul, his closet was bursting with clothes, and the last time he counted, he owned thirty-one pairs of shoes. He had never thought of them as a burden. To the contrary, they were the whole point.

'Where are you from, if I may ask?' she asked.

When Alan, still wrapped up in his thoughts, didn't answer at once, she thought about it.

'Of course. You're Kurdish. I forgot. I am speaking Turkish to you. Would you prefer Persian?' she asked in Farsi.

Again, he was taken aback.

'Pleased to have you as my neighbour?' she said in Arabic.

'Turkish is good,' he said, amazed by her magical ability.

'The neighbourhood used to be better. Now there are so many transients here. My neighbours in this flat never stay more than a few weeks, then they disappear. But perhaps they don't leave, and I just don't recognize them. Someday I'll run into my son, and won't know it. Unless he speaks to me, then I'll recognize him instantly. It's his exterior that would fool me. I'm sure he's wearing all sorts of strange clothing. Religious fanatics do. I don't know if I told you – he was constitutionally a fanatic. As a teenager, he believed passionately in the superiority of his school. I hate all institutions, but I kept my mouth shut. He ran the dance committee as if it was higher office.' Her eyes were wide open, and full of tears. 'Then he went to college, and became a Leninist. A Leninist in America. He came home to harangue. He called his father a capitalist pig because he speculated on the stock market. One day at college, during lunch, he jumped up on the dining-room table as if it was a barricade, and sang a Russian revolutionary song. His Russian was excellent. Someone made a photo of him. It was in all the newspapers: an angel singing and waving his fist, his face hysterical. His blond hair was like a halo around his delicate face. He was really a male version of me. Then, later, after he dropped out of college and the revolution failed, he joined a sect. They assigned him a young girl to marry. I did not like her. How could I? She was utterly primitive. Very thin. And played the recorder. One day he showed up here and asked me for money. For the order. To publish religious pamphlets.'

As she spoke, her hands were fumbling at the side of the table. Finally she pulled open a drawer, and removed a box of salty crackers. The box had been squashed in there, and it was nearly empty. She rummaged at the bottom, and found a small piece, which she stuffed into her mouth.

'Crackers,' she said, 'crackers are good if you have to cry. They soak up your feelings.' After a minute, when the cracker had worked, she continued. 'My son was asking us for money to support a religious cause. My son knew how much I hate religion. It was a slap in my face. He sat here lecturing us about the meaning of life, and demanding, again and again, money for his sect. My husband said, "Why don't you do something sensible with my money?" My husband had a dream of investing in a gas station.' She found a last cracker in the box, and ate it hastily. 'And my son began rolling up our carpets, the carpets we had bought in Istanbul. Beautiful carpets. They were the only possessions I really loved. Each one meant something different to me. His father just sat in his chair and watched. I tried to stop him, our big son. But he was much stronger than me, he squeezed my arms, and pushed me away. I had to watch him roll them up, and fold them. His hands were full, so he kicked the door shut behind him. I shouted after him, "A curse on you if I ever see you again!"

'I saw the bruises on my arms for weeks. I never did see my son again. It was reasonable enough for him to stay away – after what I said, he really couldn't come back.

'Once, when his father was very ill, he called me. He said he was with the Hari Krishna. He tried me for money. They needed it. I said nothing. He kept saying, "Hello? Hello?" His tone got angrier and angrier. I just listened to that voice. After a while, he hung up. I look for him on the street sometimes. One day, one of those men in orange will come forward to me and say, "Hello, Mama." Have some more sherry, please. I must not forget to be a good hostess.'

He had not wondered why she could speak Turkish, but she evidently expected such a question.

'My husband was an Orientalist. He taught in Vienna. When the Nazis came, we moved to Istanbul. My husband had relations there. Our son was born there. What do you do?' When Alan didn't answer she went on, 'You look like a gentleman. What do you do?'

Alan thought it over.

'I am an actor.'

Mrs Allen was so pleased.

'Well, you know you and my husband are really

colleagues. My husband worked as an elevator man on Park Avenue. He always said his job gave him much more time to think than his university position ever had. He was never very good with his hands but good enough to press levers and open the gate and then the door. He wore big gloves. I have kept them. Nearly all of the tenants treated him with the utmost respect. Because he never let on. He behaved like the perfect uneducated doorman. He was actually well-off because of a little hobby he had. The stock market. He came home from work and said, "My tenants don't suspect I have five times, ten times, the money they do." We never spent it. It amused us in the abstract. A large number can be very satisfying.'

*   *   *

She had opened another box of crackers.

'I imagine what you'll find hardest to get used to here is the constant praying. The politicians are worse than the clergy, it's God this and God that, all day long, and the most intelligent people don't mind. There is a clearer separation of Church and State in Turkey. I had such a shock when we moved to the United States, and I looked at my first coin. There is written, "In God we trust." You can't even buy a piece of chewing gum without having the word God pass over your palm. And who is "we", anyway? Yesterday there was a fire in a factory in Chicago, so the President went on national radio and television, and he said, "I can only promise the bereaved – tonight, all Americans are praying for you." Well, I wasn't praying. Does that mean I'm not an American?' She took a cracker, her voice quavering. 'My husband defended this American peculiarity. He said the American didn't believe in God any more than I did, that God was just a slogan to them, meaning decency and good luck, and what was wrong with that. Once we argued so loudly about America that the neighbours called the police. We had such a laugh. Then he died, and I have been writing God stories. As a way of keeping the argument going. But now I am boring you to extinction.'

'I suppose your interest is Middle Eastern politics. America sold the Kurds down the river. I guess you know that.'

When Alan did not reply, she went on, but it was all about America arming the Iraqi Kurds and encouraging them to fight for a homeland, just to keep Saddam Hussein busy on his western border, which Alan didn't wish to hear about. He stood up in the middle of a long complex sentence, and went to see her living room. It resembled her kitchen. The floors were bare, the walls covered by books. A double bed stood squarely in the middle of the room, an old radio next to it. A television was wedged under one of the bookshelves. The only books he kept in his apartment in Istanbul was the telephone book. But he admired learning. She came up behind him, apologizing for having bored him. He pointed at the television.

'May I?' he asked, as he switched it on.

'Oh no, please,' she protested, half-heartedly. She didn't want to offend her guest. Canned laughter came from the television. She listened. Someone was telling a long joke. Then she laughed. 'It's quite funny, really.' She moved closer. She stood in front of the television. She laughed again. 'I had no idea television could be so funny,' she said. 'Let's watch a little. It is called a sitcom. You're supposed to sit down to watch it.'

And so it came to pass that Alan and Mrs Allen spent the evening watching various sitcoms together. They did not sit down, because she did not want to concede her interest, and he did not want to be impolite. They hovered in front of the set. Finally Alan tired of it. The room offered no other distractions. Just those overflowing bookcases. And an old photograph propped up on a nightstand next to her bed. It showed a strong young man holding on his shoulders a small boy with long thick blond curls. She had no extra possessions, no souvenirs, which Alan considered essential for comfort.

'I must go,' he said. She turned off the television, laughing ruefully. 'Horrible stuff. But watching with you is amusing. If I had grandchildren, I would have to watch with them. I'm sure I do have grandchildren. My son must have children by now. I will never get to know them. In the ancient literature, when the mother finds out that her son is evil, she decides to die. But I decided to live.'

He did not care for the word evil. Nor did he care what anybody else thought about dying, much less what an old person might think. In Istanbul, old age was considered unfashionable, and those afflicted by it kept to themselves. He had not considered them of any use, but not a particular nuisance, either; he rarely had anything to do with them professionally, and they were not part of his social circle. He had forgotten them. But Mrs Allen had strange abilities. He wondered whether they came with old age.

63

'Bye bye. Thank you,' he said and edged towards the door. He didn't want to watch her clean up after him.

'I guess you are a busy man,' she said. 'But so am I a busy woman. Nevertheless, I hope we will see each other again.'

He looked at her intently. His expression reassured her, that he had enjoyed himself and would come again. When he reached his own door, the phone rang and it was Mr Ballinger asking him about his day. He said it had been very interesting, but didn't go into details. He said he was on schedule, and America wasn't a problem, and then he hung up.

A few years earlier, he had turned down an invitation to work in America. The job was well paid, but he had had no desire to travel. A colleague of his was hired instead, flew to New York from Istanbul for just one day, pretending to be a businessman with an appointment – well, he really was a businessman with an appointment. He had an address in New York, street, house, apartment number, and all he had to do was ring the bell, shoot the man who answered, and then take the next taxi to the airport. This assassin, like Alan, couldn't speak a word of English. But that didn't account for his mistake. A woman, not a man, opened the door, and there were another five people in the living room. He shot them all, to be on the safe side. Of course, the authorities never dreamed that he might be connected to the crime, and he returned home safely. His employers were irritated with him – he had mixed up the apartment numbers. They had to hire someone else. No doubt reports of this botched job had circulated, and that was why Alan's employers had given him a few extra days to get to know his victims. So thought Alan, beginning his third night as an unarmed man in America.

*   *   *

So, what do you do as an unarmed man without a television or a radio or even a comic book or a gun magazine in a town where you don't know anyone but yourself? You amuse yourself. The possibilities are endless for someone like Alan, whose body was a trusted companion to his brain. His *Kir* was always on the alert for amusement, always eager. Alan had heard men complain about the laziness and unreliability of these companions, but his never rested. When Alan lay down on his cot, his *Kir* promised a long-distance shot that would put a mark on the ceiling, like a *gifkafti*. Alan pictured how, after he had moved out, after finishing his job, that mark would secretly mock Mr Ballinger. The *Kir* did not like thoughts of Mr Ballinger and began to sulk.

Alan apologized and mentally fetched one of the girls who had turned down his advances years earlier. She was a sweet girl, who had something precious to give to a husband. Alan had not succeeded in persuading her to release this to him. Thus, she gave it to him again and again in countless different ways and moods, over the years, in his imagination. She was always reluctant and shy, he a bit contemptuous. He particularly enjoyed taking her from behind, with the rest of her flailing in protest. This was a zone not protected by family rites, a *Kir* could travel there without having a levy of marriage imposed. There was no envelope to rip open just once, only to find inside the letter of the law. The law was family honour. And he who violated this, paid with his life.

The *qunek* did not suffer the same sanctions as the *kus*, but it was nevertheless quite a task to reach. Because it was surrounded by a great curved obstacle, the two clenched slabs of the *qun*. The stronger these slabs, the harder it was to push them aside, the greater was a *Kir's* natural longing to succeed. Occasionally, a girl was willing, and a young man did not have to resort to force. He was free to adore the *qunek*, its colouring – a good carpet from Van sometimes has this intensity of colour. Nothing could stop him now from pushing further, into the narrow temple that lay beyond. On entering, he was nearly overwhelmed by incense, a mixture of smells, sweet and acrid. In this remote place, harmony and disharmony merged, producing huge waves of sensation, unbearably strong feelings of attraction and disgust that clashed violently, as did the pleasurable but painful pressures on something that did not fit easily inside, and was quickly, briefly, squeezed to a pulp.

The *Kir* aimed for the ceiling. It splashed the wall next to the bed.

Alan had devoted his interest, since his childhood, to the *qun*. He had seen them bare for the first time when he peeked and saw his older sister crouched in the outhouse at home. But as her body was strictly off limits to him, the boy's interest had been naturally drawn to the less well-protected *qunek* of the local ladies – the donkeys, chickens and sheep. In fact, his very first experience as a man was with a beautiful brown ewe. One day, during the long summer school break, he had been sent to visit his grown-up cousin, a shepherd. They had spend a pleasant morning together, and as the day wore on and he grew restless, his cousin said, 'Why don't you try her, over there? She's really nice.' He spent a few weeks with his cousin, and was never bored. Back at home with his grandmother, he discovered a news-paper ad for plane travel. A stewardess wearing a tight uniform, with what looked like a paper hat, pointed at a globe. The skirt reached just below her knees. A stretch of calf was visible, and an ankle disappearing into a pump. The ad was in black-and-white but he imagined the whiteness of that calf, its nudity. When he could no longer contain his admiration, he ran to see the family donkey. She was old and never baulked. He held up her tail with one hand, studied the stewardess with the other, and had his way with the donkey. One day, a villager appeared in the field. The boy was caught *in flagrante*. He waited with bowed head while the elderly man headed straight towards him with heavy footsteps. But all he wanted was to see the picture. He was not angry – children will be children. When Alan grew older, he too much preferred women.

Alan was lying on the bed, enjoying the view of a puddle on the wall. High-quality stuff, he praised himself. Then an odd thought intruded. A man only had so much fluid in his body. Possibly, this was a limited amount. He had spent enormous amounts of it in his youth, really he had squan-dered it. Was it possible, that at some point, the body couldn't produce any more? He decided to turn over a new leaf, and become thrifty in this respect. Abstinence was a sign of strong character. He felt proud of himself in advance.

His thoughts turned to his work. He recalled his very first murder. The victim was a cock. The bird had a crown of pink flesh on its head, and it had won all five of its last cock fights, bearing no scars of battle at all. This was his father's favourite possession. The boy had twisted its head, around and around. The cock did not protest, it was already weak. Alan had never been afraid to die through someone else's hand. At the same time, he was absolutely sure that he, unlike his parents, would die in a bed. This did not put him off beds, either. He thought of dying as something perfectly ordinary, like breathing and then not breathing. He saw no pathos in it. Certainly he was not afraid of it. The cock was a symbol to him of a harmonious death. He often thought of it. He had strangled it after his father died. First, he had broken its wing so he could justify the act to his grandmother as mercy killing. He knew his father would want to have that bird with him, wherever he was.

FOUR

THE NEXT MORNING BEGAN with confusion: when he woke up, he did not recognize the room. He looked around in bewilderment, at the dingy walls, at the plastic furniture and the dirty window, until the mark on the wall reminded him of his handiwork, and his orientation returned in a rush of pride and then regret. He admonished himself to be abstemious, from now on. And to concentrate on his job. He would get up now. The bed's current pulled him down. He made swimming motions. Finally, he reached over to his trousers neatly folded on the floor next to the bed, and pulled his pocket mirror from a back pocket. Floating on his back, he reviewed the lines in his forehead, around his lustrous black eyes, and a sag that he had been following around his cheeks, that interfered with the vitality of his four-day-old *simbêltûj*. Its margins were becoming clearer. His hair lay in a thin fuzz on the pillow. Mortality did not become him. Vanity helped him jump out of bed, scoot to the bathroom. As he was shaving, his discontent grew, and on impulse he snipped off the ends of his moustache, turning it into a *simbêltapan*. He would allow the middle to grow in again. Better. He set out for the donut shop.

Weather: fair and seasonably cold. Pat was working the morning shift. He ordered 'One donut, and coffee, please' – nearly a complete sentence – and waited to receive accolades. Her disdain was so great that she did not even seem to recognize him, did not ask him to pay the debt he had incurred on his first night, did not acknowledge his mastery of English, did not return the compliment of his smile. He did not stay to watch her work, but humbly took his breakfast to go.

In fact, he felt slightly weakened from last night's activities. His legs felt wobbly, as if they had lost muscle. Then he chastened himself, it wasn't overexertion but duty neglected that made a man fragile. In three days on the job, he had still not set foot in the house, had no idea in which room he would take care of his subjects. He was supposed to surprise them after nightfall, after the man of the house had left for Istanbul. So he needed to find his way around the house in total darkness. When an assassin wants a job to be neat, he has to understand the locality exactly, where the beds are positioned, how the closets open and close. He has to find in advance several hiding places for himself, and at least one extra way out if things go wrong. And he has to know where the bathroom is, for afterwards – inevitably, he has to use the facilities.

Alan Korkunc was fastidious about his work, self-critical. He kept himself under complete control too – he denied his pulse the right to speed up. Occasionally, it did anyway, to his annoyance. By planning a job in advance, down to the most minor detail, one minimizes surprises, and one does not have to feel anything. While killing someone, Alan was like a bank teller counting change, or a grocer packing up vegetables.

To this end, he headed towards his accustomed slot in the front of the house. He kept the windows of his taxi open, and the breeze came in with such vigour that his ears and nose turned bright red. As he turned the corner of the subject's street, he saw the children coming down the front steps with the maid, Tuerkan. She staggered under the weight of a sleigh, while the children pranced ahead. He accelerated, swooshing by, hoping she had not noticed him. His pulse beat in double time.

The street ended in a park just a block away. He stopped there, and watched Tuerkan approaching with the children. He saw her glance at the taxi from afar, and he pulled away from the kerb again. He drove aimlessly. Finally, inspiration came, like a tardy guest, bearing a gift. He drove all the way home again.

His namesake was not at all surprised when he rang the doorbell. She welcomed him into her kitchen, began moving papers aside to make room for her traditional lunch. She was wielding a tin of sardines when he put his hand on her wrist. He shook his head.

'No, *Xalti*,' he said. *Xalti* means venerated aunt. He produced his most beguiling smile. 'Can you help me pull the donkey out of the mire?' he asked.

71

'My gosh, I am flattered,' she said, still holding the tin. 'No one's needed my help in a long time.' She seemed nailed to the floor, though. She just stood there staring at him, examining his smile.

He relaxed the corners of his mouth a little, gently took the tin of sardines from her hand, and added, 'I'll buy you lunch somewhere else.'

Her pink coat hung on the back of a chair. He held it out for her, like a gentleman. She knew its contours, and slipped inside with agility. He helped her down the stairs. He had left the taxi double-parked in front of the house.

She wanted to sit in the front next to him, but he shook his head, and asked her to sit in the back, 'like a proper passenger'.

She seemed disappointed, but did as he asked.

'You better turn on the meter or you'll get arrested for driving me around with the meter turned off,' she called from the back seat.

She leaned forwards, and showed him how. He had not thought of that. Having the meter running and a passenger in the back brought him instant relief from the pedestrians.

She talked. She told him that driving was her one thwarted ambition. She had always wanted to drive. But her husband had not believed in driving. He said, 'Do we drive a subway car, or a bus? That's right, we leave that to someone else. And we can leave driving cars to someone else too.' A week after her husband died, she applied for a learner's permit. She was seventy by then.

'In America,' she told Alan, 'cars are a form of outdoor

clothing. People get into their cars, the way they get into a coat. I am naked without a car.'

She took driving lessons, but failed her driving test after making a few small mistakes. She said she made mistakes when the examiner was in the car, because he didn't believe she could drive, he made her nervous, he distracted her, it was the examiner's fault. She failed the driving test seven times.

'Because they're prejudiced against old age,' she complained. 'They wouldn't even know I was old – if it wasn't for my white hair.'

'I'll teach you how to drive some day,' he promised.

'You don't need to,' she replied. 'I can drive. The state won't allow me to. Not yet.'

He drove slowly around the park near the subject's house, until he spotted the children riding pell-mell on the sleigh down a slope, and Tuerkan watching them from the top of the hill, her posture describing tense despair. Alan drove back to the house. He told his passenger that he had to run an errand. If the police came, she was to shoo them away with an excuse – the driver was fetching her heart medicine, something like that.

'I don't need heart medicine. My hands don't even shake. I'll think of something better,' she agreed. 'I'll tell them you're buying me something to read. I haven't had the newspaper yet.'

'Later,' he promised.

He left her there, inside the running taxi, with the blinker on. He strode to the front door. The telephone was ringing inside the house. No one answered it. He trotted up the stairs, and used his key to enter the house. Tuerkan had neglected to turn on the burglar alarm, so he had no further duties and could devote himself to exploring the house.

*   *   *

Alan always found entering people's houses the most disagreeable part of his job. Remember, he didn't like to go to other people's homes. Once he had passed the threshold, he became too engaged with the task at hand to mind being on a kind of visit. He even took a professional interest in furnishings, planning his hits to fit them in. He had worked in some fancy houses. If he had been asked to kill 'with maximum footprint', he made sure he didn't catch his victims standing on a beautiful old carpet. Leather furniture was an exception: the more expensive it was, the easier it was to clean. The Erkal house proved to have wall-to-wall carpeting, which Alan considered unhygienic and tasteless, mass-produced. The living room had an expanse of carpet white as a fresh page of paper. It was asking for a crimson signature.

The sofa came in sections that seated at least eight, its cushions so plush that they looked hazardous. A small child could suffocate there. A possibility. That had never been done before in his trade. Word would get around. He pictured the effect on a father strolling in. The glass coffee table looked fragile – Alan made a note to avoid commotion in its vicinity.

A praying carpet lay over the back of the sofa. He regarded it with new-found disdain, seeing it with Mrs Allen's eyes.

He wondered whether it had been done before in New York – the death scene with victim on the prayer carpet, it was a worn motif in Turkey. Probably Sulymon had heard of it. And it wouldn't look good with a woman. He had exhausted the possibilities of the living room, and returned to the hall.

He skirted the stairway going up to the second floor, and entered the guest toilet. Very handy. Interesting floral room scent. Expensive toilet paper. On the far end of the hall was a dining room, with more white wall-to-wall carpeting and another glass table, this one big enough to hold a victim – a possibility. Swinging doors led to a kitchen. The kitchen had a television attached to the ceiling, and gadgets that interested Alan. He would have some time after finishing his job to see what they had. There were sure to be some surprises, new technology that hadn't reached the highest echelons of Istanbul. He noted the back door to a small garden. There were a number of windows. He would have to turn off the lights if someone was in the kitchen. Possibly Tuerkan. Luckily, there was a switch at the back door. Alan decided not to bring in the cutting knife he would need to trim the ears and the rubber glove to hold them, but take these utensils from the owner. The gloves had an appointed place at the sink, right next to a knife holder. Alan's memory was excellent and he would have no trouble finding his way around the kitchen in the dark.

He returned to the hall, and ascended the stairs. The domain upstairs was colourful, but neat. A nursery had two small beds, a large television, toys and dolls and its own bathroom with Mickey Mouse toothbrushes hung above the

75

sink. He would do the children in their beds. No reason for them to know what was going on. Further along a small corridor lined with cupboards – towels in there he might need – was another bathroom, and another bedroom with a bombastic black bed, matching wardrobes and dressers, another television, another bathroom, with black tiles. He had never used a black toilet before.

He was counting bathrooms. Four bathrooms, and two bedrooms. That was luxury. He would have the same some-day. If Ajda Erkal was in the bed, he could take care of her there. She would not be wearing high-heeled shoes, so nothing would distract him. He warned himself not to look for the shoes before finishing his work. He imagined enter-ing, seeing the shoes before the bed, and losing precious milliseconds staring at them, while their owner started a dreadful commotion. As he was returning downstairs, the peace and quiet of his visit was marred by a loud ringing. It was the phone in his pocket.

Mr Ballinger.

'So how are you, and where are you exactly?'

'Fine, thank you.'

He was breaking the lock of the back door, carefully, so that no one would notice, and pulled the door shut behind him. Mr Ballinger must be watching him somehow.

'Well, I'll call you when you're not so busy,' Mr Ballinger said.

The back-garden walk had not been properly cleared of snow. The help was not doing its job. His shoes were getting muddy. He made a hasty exit, nodding at the cold house walls: he would be back in two days, under different circumstances.

*   *   *

'*Xalti*,' he said. '*Xalti*, help me find Fifth Avenue and Tenth Street.'

'First the newspaper, please,' she said.

She didn't need to look at a map. She pointed, he followed, they reached Fifth Avenue and he drove as slowly as possible because he saw all the shoppers, and he felt left out.

'If only I had some time to buy a few things,' he remarked, his voice tragic. 'I've been wearing the same outfit for days.'

'Clothes are shackles,' she said. 'Be glad you are free of them.'

'And books,' he asked, 'and papers – are they not shackles too?'

'You're right, of course,' she said. 'Funny, I never think of them that way. But you're absolutely right. I shall get rid of them.'

'No, don't!' he said, horrified. 'Your books are beautiful. There's a newspaper stand.'

The Avenue became more modest and his envy diminished. Tenth Street was nothing special. Sulymon Erkal's store had a large window filled with Oriental antiques. He pulled right in front. He saw Sulymon behind a counter, looking like any salesman, and as fat as one of the miller's chickens. He was facing a customer, whose back was turned towards the door. Alan recognized the pin-striped suit and the thick greying hair instantly. Mr Ballinger. He backed up, until the taxi was hidden from sight.

77

'Read the newspaper, *Xalti*,' he said. 'I'll be right back.'
She was staring at the paper, one eye tightly shut.

He crossed the street and watched from afar. Sulymon had been a lean man once, he had looked hungry all the time, and his dangling ears had made him look canine. Now he looked well-fed and satisfied. He had some hair-loss at the temples, not much, he had wrinkles, but not many. He concealed his jowls with a yellow scarf. And he was annoyed. His mouth opened and shut rapidly, he poked his chin forwards and stared at Mr Ballinger, who lifted his hand in a placating gesture. Then Mr Ballinger picked up a package he was holding between his legs. He held it up to Sulymon, whose face altered. Anger subsided. The businessman seemed to be unsure of himself. Finally, he came out in front of the counter, and shook Mr Ballinger's hand. He accepted the package, returned with it to the desk, and tore it open, with childish eagerness. Inside were two giant teddy bears. Mrs Allen's face was turned towards the newspaper on her lap, but both her eyes were shut, or he might have asked her opinion. Now Sulymon was apparently thanking Mr Ballinger. They conversed for a while, until Mr Ballinger showed him a newspaper clipping. Sulymon got angry all over again, and they began to argue. Their hands waved and landed in fists on the table. Mr Ballinger slammed the newspaper on the desk, grabbed his coat from a chair, and left the store abruptly. He did not bother to put on his coat, anger heating him sufficiently. He walked directly into the street. His eyes dwelt briefly on Alan's cab, but before he could study it, another taxi pulled up next to him, he got in, and was driven away. Alan crossed the street again, and loitered on the kerb one car-length from Sulymon's shop. The limousine pulled up.

Sulymon was locking the store. He carried the box with the two dolls. The snow lay deep on the ground. He passed Alan. His Italian loafers, treading on the snow, squeaked.

Squeaking boots on snow had been the first sound the boy heard over a roar in his ears after he nearly drowned in a snow bank, and a soldier lifted him free. As the soldier carried him upside down back to his grandmother, the roar in the boy's ears settled into a pounding, and the squeaking continued. Ever since his mother died, his grandmother had looked after him. His father, his Bavo, was away that day, taking care of the livestock. Bavo had gone to market and did not know about the little boy's predicament, evidently did not feel it in his bones, did not return home early, did not even return home on time. Instead, he really did not return home at all. The next morning, while the boy was eating grandmother's fresh bread for breakfast, and listening to her scold and chafe, he heard boots squeaking on the snow again, but this time many of them. He did not bother to interrupt his grandmother formally, he simply sprang up and ran to the door. His uncles and neighbours stood framed in the doorway. This time they were carrying someone else, someone heavy, whose weight they shared among their big bare red hands. It was Bavo.

A week before, Bavo had already had bad luck. He had been standing at attention with the other farmers while the national anthem was played on the crowded market square.

But then, one of his sheep had broken loose, wandered away. He gave chase. Five soldiers thrashed him, while the brass band did not lose a beat of the national anthem. A week later, another form of local bedlam had broken out. A member of the Bruki clan had insulted a member of the malevolent Cumki clan – to be specific, the owner of the tobacco shop on the town square had accused one of his employees of stealing. A lot of yelling and screaming was followed by scampering feet and then silence, as the town square emptied, and beyond, people scrambled for cover. Then the stones began to fly. Stones hailed in all directions through town. Alan's grandmother put an end to the non-sense. It was assumed, in that part of the world, that old age brings stamina, wisdom, courage. Old women were in charge of washing the dead. They were in charge, period. Fearlessly, she chugged over the mounds of snow on the street, holding up her long black skirts, till she reached the town square, the epicentre of this outrage.

She posted herself there, her hands in the air, and yelled, 'Stop! At once!'

As instantly as it had begun, the fight stopped. Men put down their stones and went back to work, children came out of their houses and went back to their games. In the dusk, Alan went to his post. His grandmother was waiting for both her men when Alan slipped into a snow bank and was rescued by a soldier. But Bavo did not return home from work that evening. He was found at daylight lying between two carts in a gutter; a stone had caught him on the back of the head, no one saw him fall, and he had frozen to death.

The shoes that squeaked on a Manhattan street belonged to a man who had worn military boots in Kurdistan. They reminded Alan of Bavo's face, how it looked after being found, his jaw wide open, the gums still raw where his teeth had been knocked out a week earlier.

He began to wonder what Mr Ballinger was doing at Sulymon's office, and what the quarrel might be about. Then he reprimanded himself: it was none of his business. Mr Ballinger's motives for punishing Sulymon were utterly beside the point. They were no doubt political in nature. The two must be dividing the world among themselves. Let them. He had a job to do.

*   *   *

Later, when our hero no longer needed Mrs Allen's services, he brought her home. He put on his best manners for her, as if they were a costume. They covered up the annoyance that had broken out in him, like a horrible itchy contact rash. This was not Mrs Allen's fault. He always had this reaction when he spent too much time with another person. Still, he waited with professional courtesy in her doorway while she thanked him for the excursion, he waited some more while she invited him for dinner, waited, after he shook his head, until she had finished her speech of regret. At last she said goodbye, and ended his term of waiting. He stepped back, his irritability already soothed by watching the black metal door swing shut. As he turned away, he noticed something. A vertical shaft of light ran along one side of his own door. A crack in the door. What does that mean? It had not been closed properly. Someone else had passed through the door in his absence. Without thinking, he backed away. Time enough to find out why his door was open. Possibly, someone was still inside. Perhaps the janitor. Or Mr Ballinger. Why hadn't they provided him with a gun?

He strolled over to Broadway and walked upriver. Red, white and blue refuse tossed along the sidewalk and swirled in the gutters. *Jam-jam* everywhere. On the far side of the street, there were fewer. He crossed over. More *jam-jam* there, convivial, at home. Too much trouble trying to avoid them. There were other hazards. Many sidewalks in New York have metal grates. These are gills, they allow the city to breathe. I hope you never have to experience New York exhaling, in great hot breaths stinking of train tracks and chewing gum. The earth shudders and rumbles. The city times itself, waits for a girl to pass by, then it breathes out suddenly, and tears the girl's skirt above her head. When a New Yorker talks about being 'streetwise', he is referring to the experienced way a resident avoids sidewalk grates. But Alan didn't, and his coat swept about him in a rude fashion, as though the town was making fun of the flimsy cloth. If his nerves were audible, they would have added to the din. As he came up the side of the road, he saw Oriental spires and a dome. A mosque.

He slowed down. The steel fire door had a quiet, welcoming dignity. He heeded the invitation. He entered, planning to kneel on the rugs next to the other men, bend his head down with them, speak to fate, ask what it had in mind, that sort of thing, perhaps make a few suggestions. Pray. An uncle had taken him along just once, as a child, flattering him. He had enjoyed going through the motions with the other men, kneeling with them. But he found it even more enjoyable to join the grown men in a coffee house, leaping up and shouting while they watched a football game on the only town television. In any case, his uncle must have found this child unsuitable religious material, because he never invited him along again. Forty years later, he entered a mosque of his own free will. Why not? Nobody he knew was watching.

He could make out swinging doors in the dark entrance hall, and pushed through them into a gloomy room. It took him a while to realize that the congregation was positioned in rows at one side of the room. He slid into the nearest empty chair. He kept his attention to himself. He did not look around. But he did not pray either. If you force a contented man into contemplation, he inevitably thinks about all that could go wrong, while the discontented man thinks about all that should go right. They become more equal. But Alan was schooled through his work: he did not think about himself. For a while, he just existed: a man in a chair.

He hated sitting. When he became aware of his buttocks, he glanced around at his surroundings. In the middle of the room, facing the worshippers, stood a most peculiar man. He was impossibly dressed, in a formless black robe, with what looked like a miner's lamp on his head, another tied around his upper arm. His lower arms were wrapped in white sheets, which he continuously tugged, wrapping and unwrapping them. The holy book stood open on a stand before him. The floor looked mean, hard and bare. Alan's hearing kicked in, and he heard the man singing in what he took to be Arabic. It sounded different in the New World, but he was not fond of that language. He enjoyed the Turkish habit of contemptuously calling Arabs, *Arap*, which means black-skinned but also primitive. The worshippers rocked back and forth, their eyes closed. They all wore the same sheets around their arms, the miner's tool around their foreheads, and identical little hats. A uniform. Alan hated uniformity of any kind. And he knew what Mrs Allen would say. He stood up loudly, scraping his chair, not caring. On his way out, he saw the Star of David in the entrance hall. He decided to spend some money. Perhaps he could purchase a gun.

There were general shops, and specialty shops for every conceivable consumer good, but not one carried guns. America's excellent reputation in the trade was clearly wildly exaggerated; the little he knew about the place was proving wrong. He put his hand on the left side of his chest, where he understood his heart to be, and held it there, a bit of additional support. He lingered in front of a men's store. It occurred to him in a new burst of woe that several weeks had passed in which he had not bought himself any new clothes at all. His tailor-made suits were orphaned in Istanbul. No one else would dare to wear them. He hadn't thought about it before: whether the police had vandalized his possessions, or divided them among themselves. Perhaps the *kapüçe* had gotten to them first, and now owned thirty-one pairs of shoes! He was a tiny man with a glass eye, who once, while polishing Alan's shoes, confided in him about his collection of Western-label brassières. He had worked in an international youth hostel, and could select carefully, over the course of years, from the suitcases of his guests.

Alan's need to buy himself something new became urgent. He entered the store. The employees skulked in the background, so he looked at the suits hanging on a rack. They were factory-sewn, coarse material, much like his overcoat. Never mind. He took one off the rack, a bright-green three-piece suit. An atrociously dressed salesman approached, pointed the only customer to a curtained-off closet. It had a long mirror. Alan looked at himself and gave critique. The moustache was turning out splendidly. The figure less so: he had lost muscle tone, after abruptly ending his weight-lifting regimen. He dropped his trousers and lambasted his legs – you look like you belong on a little boy! His *Kir* hid. Quickly, he put on the green trousers. Much too large, *canê*, he said to himself tenderly. But the cheap jacket looks nice. Builds up those sharp-edged shoulders, which are broad anyway. Green. Bold. He did not bother looking at the price; he never did. If he ever wanted something, he paid what it cost and did not think about it twice. But he was unsure about the green, whether it wasn't in bad taste – it was the Islamic colour – and he left the shop without buying it.

He intended to return home, but his legs, bowing to some insecurity and trembling a little, refused to co-operate, and delivered him to a haberdashery. He tried on a series of hats,

85

which were all much too small, to his disappointment, until he noticed the salesgirls standing in a bunch of pretty faces laughing at him, and he realized that they were women's hats. All of America was laughing at him.

Again, he turned towards home. He felt very peculiar. He could not define this feeling because it had no recognizable contours – it wasn't a bellyache or a cramp. It was a black trickle of a mood that seeped from his mind into his stomach, and carried part of his stomach into his limbs. His legs continued to carry him at quite a clip the wrong way up Broadway. He was practically running. He managed to stop himself at a grocery store. There, he ignored fruits he had never seen before, which means under normal circumstances he would have desired them – they had exotic, expensive names such as papaya, and mango. Instead, he bought some lowly bananas and apples, and took great pleasure in their charms. He had quite a number of large bills still left in his wallet, and his legs under control again.

Still no gun shops. The city panted through a sidewalk grate. He identified the entrance to the subway. A subway could take him somewhere else. But he had never, ever, set foot inside one. He had never even been to see the Istanbul *tünel*, although it was the object of intense civic pride, an ancient ornament. He did not care for old things. Ankara had a brand-new subway, but that nearly ended his career.

He had stupidly accepted a job in Ankara which required him to take care of his subject in public, in the subway, at rush hour. He finished his task just as the train pulled into the station and opened its doors. The crowd, heaving the assassin and his dead victim along, pushed them both into the train, pinned them together there at the door, while the train rumbled on. He nearly fainted with apprehension about being locked in, and barely made it out at the next stop. The dead man was trampled as the doors opened and everyone assumed, when his body was finally noticed, that he had died after suffering a coronary and the subsequent stomping – the job was not successful as a public execution.

Alan felt this episode did not count as an instance of taking the subway, and he continued to brag that he had never, ever set foot on public transport in his whole adult life. The last time he had seen the inside of a bus was for the journey from his town near Mount Ararat to Istanbul. His grandmother had brought him and his small plastic suitcase to the bus station, her face soggy from weeping. He had not cried once, not until the bus pulled out of town. He cried the two days and nights it took to reach Istanbul. He was just fifteen. His uncle was supposed to meet him in Istanbul, and when he didn't show up, the boy dried his eyes and made do. In truth, Alan hadn't waited one minute to see where his uncle might be standing. As soon as the bus arrived, he ducked into the crowd. His uncle was a street vendor. He had arthritis, and wanted the boy to take over his job peddling melons. Alan never saw or spoke to his grand-mother again. He had broken his promise to call her. He always planned to return in style, his Mercedes packed full of presents. But he had never found the time. Now he had time, in bulk, like stored rotten fruit, and that was his wealth.

Just thinking about buses produced a bus terminal, a chunk of dark grimy building looming on the next block. Was fate giving him a hint? Alan went inside, and studied the arrivals and departures board. He clutched his bag of food like a talisman. It was his, his to save or consume. It would last him a day, and a day was enough surely to get somewhere else. He could hop on a bus and leave. Disappear. But where to? The only name he recognized on the big board was Washington, because the only American city he had ever heard of, besides the capital and New York, was Hollywood. It wasn't listed. His disappointment ached. At the very least, he knew America as those three place-names, but if Hollywood was not a place you could visit, then he knew that much less what America was. Someone had gone into his apartment.

He had never suffered any burst of intuition that others reported, when something bad was about to happen. His arrest had come without the slightest warning. But now he felt something nudging him, poking at his nerves, a sensation he could only ascribe to instinct. He left the bus terminal and when he passed a movie house, he went in. He had generally only gone to the movies to amuse his *Kir*, but now he could hardly enquire whether this film would be suitable. He took his chances. And was disappointed – it proved to be one of those films that sometimes ran on television. A lot of dull scenery – meadows and lakes – and people talking, their faces lit up this way or that. Nobody died. The few love scenes were irritating because the couple only kissed, something he didn't like to do or watch. He only put food in his mouth, only clean food. He dozed till the movie ended. When he left the movie theatre, it was night-time. He felt relieved. He returned home.

The door still stood slightly ajar, but now he could no longer see a crack of light, so clearly the lights in his apartment were turned off. He could not imagine anyone sitting in the dark. He pushed through. He heard nothing. He switched on the lights in the hall, and then the kitchen – no one – and proceeded cautiously to the living room. No one. The lights blazing, he returned to the kitchen and saw the Turkish newspaper lying on the kitchen table. He touched it, and felt the gun inside.

He opened the newspaper. The gun lay in a leather holster directly on the black-and-white photograph of a Turkish soldier brandishing two amputated Kurdish heads. Who needs a holster? He removed the gun, his heart sinking. A Smith and Wesson. The lowest of the low. Maybe in America it was considered a better gun. It was heavy, silver and black, with a sight that glowed green in the dark. Reassured and suddenly happy, Alan pranced, waving the gun about like a dancer a handkerchief, and shaking his torso in the Kurdish manner. He sang the song of Xelef, who fought the Turks with a a sword of gold and silver, and had every reason to call himself the Greatest. Then Alan stopped. He remembered something. He removed the gun clip. It felt light to him. He opened it, and began removing the bullets, in order to count them. There were only four.

*   *   *

The assassin's favourite tool was a 32 ACP Walther. He had acquired one after his first experience with a woman. He had stood on line with his schoolmates. It was a cold afternoon, and he had kept his coat and shoes on. And then his *Kir* had fallen asleep. The woman had patted him on the head, and told him to give it a go anyway, and when it became clear that the matter was quite hopeless, she gave him his money back. It took the *Kir* several years to live this down and try again. Alan had invested the money he had saved that embarrassing afternoon to buy himself, that evening, his first Walther. He never, ever tired of the name: Walther, a German name, as glamorous as Mercedes, or BMW. He had never used another. He held the Smith and Wesson and addressed it: the Walther's four-inch barrel gives more accuracy without adding any bulk, and the double action and hammer-block safety is quick and well-nigh foolproof compared to you, stupid little American gun. The Walther has grand ballistic behaviour. I have heard that you don't, that the word ball in any form does not apply to you. The Walther's copper-jacket bullet peels back on impact while the lead core just travels on and on. This means a clean punch at close range without any splattering. And you, what can you do? You're no better than a Beretta, probably accurate to about ten feet and just strong enough to plug a vicious kitten.

He picked up the halter and flung it against the wall. A sissy American image: the killer with the halter in his armpit. Well, a Smith and Wesson probably doesn't mind getting all sweaty. He shoved the gun into the back of his trousers. It felt secure. Why only four bullets? Did they not trust him with a few extras? Or were they so sure of his ability to hit a target. He had never fired a Smith and Wesson before. Handgun skills are similar to violin skills – get a little out of practice and you lose. The assassin used to practise assiduously at home. He'd start with a .22 automatic and work up towards the heavier calibres, burning up a fair amount of ammunition in the process. And his strong handsome fingers, each with its own spine, and its own personality, were a pleasure to behold as they did their work. His hopes of finding a manicurist were diminishing.

That night, Alan trimmed his fingernails himself, using a kitchen knife. He spent the evening learning the feel of the gun, aiming at the Styrofoam cup he had set up on the table, and listening with passive interest to Mrs Allen's radio. He decided he was going to change his life, beginning with his lifestyle – from now on, he would get up early in the morning. He would be energetic. The idea of becoming a better man in this manner appealed to him. He went to bed long after the music next door had stopped.

FIVE

THE NOON SUN NUDGED him awake and showed him a new mark on the wall. His legs had the strength of untied shoelaces; he had been squandering energy again. Cold water would help. The *simbêltapan* annoyed him: a shoebox on his upper lip. He shaved off the sides, giving the moustache slanting eyes, and then divided it into two, by shaving a thin line down the middle, beneath his nose: *Simbêlnivişt*. Very dignified. All set for the day, he knocked on Mrs Allen's door.

'Another donkey stuck?' she asked, delighted.

She did not comment about the changes in his face. She flapped about the apartment, collecting her hat, coat, newspaper and a paperback book that looked dull, because the cover only had writing on it, and no picture. They drove back to Sulymon Erkal's house, but this time Alan just kept circling the block. He had not turned the meter off, and it was running high. Mrs Allen perched in the back seat, radiating contentment. She kept the book open on her lap, and her face turned to it. One of her eyes was closed, the other eye opened a crack, showing a sliver of blue. He thought she must be asleep, but every so often she turned a page.

On one of his rounds, Alan saw the red sports car pull up in front of the door. A pair of buffed brown tie shoes came out first, followed by pressed blue jeans, and a sports jacket. The bearer evidently had such vitality that he did not need a coat. His curly hair and bland face were coiffed, but his mouth and eyes had an unruly, belligerent expression. He bounded towards the front gate.

Alan turned to Mrs Allen and woke her from a reverie.

'Can you tell me whether that is an American, or a foreigner?'

The young man was just striding through the gate when above him the front door opened, and Ajda Erkal came out, looking anxious, and clearly in a hurry, because she was still slipping her arms into her little fur coat as she headed down the stairs. She had on her exquisite high heels, and her legs glistened.

The visitor's face changed the instant he saw her. The features fell into the alignment known as a soft smile. His eyes would have glowed in the dark. He reached the bottom of the staircase, he did something odd – he extended his hand. Man and woman shook hands formally. Man did not relinquish woman's hand, but turned, keeping it in his fist, and hurried her through the gate, towards his red car. He opened the car door for her. As she put one foot inside, and began her slow ascent inside the sports car, he said loudly (so loudly that her finger hopped to her lips – Shush! – but to no avail), 'You OK, Ajda?'

She nodded her head, kept her lips clenched, and swivelled her hips: she sat down.

He stood at the door, gazing down at her, and repeated sternly, 'Are you OK, my little Ajda?'

This time she called upwards, hastily, 'Yes, Davie, I'm fine.'

'I'm glad,' he said, still not moving.

'Now I am fine,' she added. 'Now I'm better.'

'That's better, my darling,' he said loudly, finally closing the car door for her.

'He's American. His name's Davie. I don't know what her name is,' Mrs Allen said, trying to be helpful.

'Her name's either Mommy or Ajda,' Alan revealed.

'Probably some call her Mommy and some Ajda,' said Mrs Allen. 'Which would you rather say to her?'

'I don't want to speak to her,' he replied.

Discreetly, he drove up behind Dave's sports car. Dave had taken control and the vehicle shot away. Alan struggled to keep up. They drove until they reached a neighbourhood that Mrs Allen said was popular with the young people. There, Dave drove into a garage, and Alan followed him. This time, he was admitted.

'Twelve dollars an hour! It's very expensive,' protested Mrs Allen.

'I have enough money,' said Alan, swerving downwards through the parking-lot corridors.

'So do I,' argued Mrs Allen, 'because I don't park my car in a garage.'

'You don't have a car,' he pointed out.

'And it's my very first time in a garage, too,' she said, pleased.

The sports car ahead of him found a space, but he did not. He wound up two flights below, and in a hurry. He helped his passenger out of the back seat, hustled her along the dark twists and turns of the corridor towards the exit – he wouldn't take the elevator, which suited her fine because she wanted to marvel at the scenery. Luckily, his quarry was dawdling on the sidewalk. They kept their heads close together, at a secretive angle Alan thought absurd, as if they were negotiating the sale of illegal goods, except that they were giggling. Every so often, Ajda looked around furtively. Then she pointed to a coffee shop. They entered.

Alan followed closely behind with Mrs Allen. The establishment was not crowded, so Alan could sit down at the booth across the aisle from the couple. He knew from experience that she would not recognize him – more than clothes, surroundings make the man. For Ajda, he was a taxi driver.

Mrs Allen studied the menu.

'Haven't you wondered that I don't need glasses?' she asked.

He had noticed but he hadn't wondered. He didn't care. She spoke about an operation, her good eye, the importance of this. And then about having lunch once a week with her bridge partners.

Ajda was holding Dave's hand under the table. Tears began spitting down her smooth cheeks. At once, Dave's hands left their hiding place beneath the table, seized a napkin, and stroked the tears with reverence. Once more, Ajda glanced around the room. Satisfied that no one was watching, she leaned forwards towards Dave, and kissed him quickly but with emphasis on the lips. Mrs Allen had turned to stare at cakes in a display case, and was of no translation help. But Alan could get the gist of the ensuing conversation, owing to the clarity of the participants' body language. You'll be wondering what they said.

Ajda Erkal was speaking softly through her tears, singing really, repeating, 'I can't stand it, I just cannot stand it.'

Dave sang back, 'One more night. Just one more night.'

Ajda protested, 'Just one more night! His last night before going away, he always wants to . . . he will kiss me . . . He will haul me into his arms. He kissed me last night, you know. On the mouth. What can I do? I'm married to him after all. I'm a polite person.'

This last information made Dave tense up visibly and he snapped at Ajda, as if he was angry with her, 'The bastard. I hope you didn't participate. What did you do?!'

Ajda Erkal laughed through her tears, lacing her hands through his on the surface of the table, for all to see.

'I told him I had my period.'

The tears ran anew, while Dave kneaded her hands. His face depicted a helpless, smug expression.

'Patience, darling,' he comforted her. 'Only one more night. And then another half a day. Then he's gone. And by the time he comes back, you'll be gone. And we'll always be together.'

'Happily ever after!' she rejoined, brightening.

Mrs Allen turned away from the cake. She picked up the menu again.

'Listen to the conversation!' he whispered, 'and explain it to me later.'

'Have you picked out what you want?' she asked. 'Where is the waiter?'

Ajda Erkal had collected herself, and her voice became dry, practical.

'I can't do all the packing myself, especially at such short notice. I'll just leave everything to the moving men. They'll arrive on Saturday afternoon, before Tuerkan leaves work. We can all move to your place Friday evening, and I'll stop by on the weekend just to make sure they've collected everything. Tuerkan will let the movers in.'

Dave did not seem to like the mention of another name.

'Who's Tuerkan?' he asked suspiciously.

Ajda seemed touched by his jealousy.

'Oh, Davie, Tuerkan's just the maid.'

Dave relaxed and said, 'Of course. Say, won't she be surprised?'

'Of course. Horrified. She adores him.'

Dave's voice clouded with suspicion.

'I bet she'll try to stop you.'

Ajda rushed to reassure him.

'Darling. How could she? Impossible. No, she will have to give him the bad news. I will tell her, that is part of her job.'

Dave was thrilled.

'Tell me, I want to hear, what you say to the bitch. In Turkish. I want to hear exactly.'

Mrs Erkal obliged him, speaking in Turkish.

'Tuerkan, *hanam*, goodbye. We're moving out. I've had enough of him, even if he's the President's friend and has all the money in the world. He'll have a little shock, but I don't want to be around to see it – I'm not a sadist.'

'OK, Davie?' she asked in English.

Dave kissed her hand passionately.

'Adorable. Your lips look so cute when you speak that gibberish. And what do you say to the old man when he begs you, when he offers to give you anything, anything at all you want to go back to him?'

Mrs Erkal broke into song.

'*Guele guele sana yolun acik olsun . . .*' (Which means: Goodbye, dear, may your path always be free.)

Dave imitated her, rocking and singing 'Blah, blah', which is what he thought she was singing.

By raising themselves from their booth seats, and leaning over the food, the happy couple could kiss, feverishly. Mrs Allen was looking at the cake, with lust in her eyes. Alan stood up abruptly, gesturing her to follow him. The kiss was not ending in the foreseeable future. Disgusting. Mrs Allen was disappointed about the cake. She took one long last look at it.

Then she observed the tangled-up couple, and whispered to Alan, 'Isn't love wonderful?' As they passed through the door she began her report: 'She's planning to leave her husband. I hope he doesn't object too much. She may be in for a terrible fright. He may break down and cry.'

Out on the street, he demanded a complete translation of the couple's conversation, and it turned out that Mrs Allen could recall it word for word.

'Why does it interest you so much?' she asked.

'Because I know her husband,' he replied.

'And do you like him?'

'Not at all,' said Alan.

'Well, in that case, she is doing the right thing,' Mrs Allen said easily. 'Shouldn't we have a piece of cake and coffee? And then I can listen some more.'

'No, no, please, *Xalti*. I want to return home.'

He was too confused to be pleasant. He was in such a quandary. He detested Sulymon Erkal and he knew that nothing, but nothing, would hurt this man more than the discovery of his wife's betrayal. He would probably hire a killer to murder her.

*   *   *

Down in the garage, Alan's phone rang. Mr Ballinger.

'Hello. How are you coming along? You don't want to join me in my club, but you seem to be visiting all sides of town.'

Alan: 'That's right. I'm getting my job done, that's what you want, isn't it?'

Mr Ballinger was not impressed.

'Tomorrow at midnight is your deadline,' he said, as if Alan might have forgotten.

'I remember. Goodbye.'

He turned to Mrs Allen who was regarding him with curiosity.

He snapped coarsely, 'Get in the car. We're leaving. We're out of fuel.'

The prospect of visiting a gas station amused her no end.

'Ah yes, gasoline!' She drew out the word 'gasoline'.

Later, while Alan filled up the tank, Mrs Allen oohed and aahed about the gas station, pointing out that the attendant was a foreigner, and the limitless possibilities of what could be sold there besides automobile products. She begged Alan to permit her to pay for fuel, as she had been travelling all over the city on his nickel, but he refused. Instead, he bought her a Coca-Cola and a ring-ding. She proclaimed the packaged chocolate pastry excellent.

*   *   *

Although he had now spent several hours in Mrs Allen's company, and was feeling restless, it was his idea to go for a walk with her. He needed shooting practice.

'Tell me, *Xalti*, are there some fields around here, without any people whatsoever?'

Mrs Allen thought about it.

'We used to go down to the little red lighthouse.'

When they reached home, she insisted on driving down into the garage with him. She forced him to take the elevator up with her, because she was too tired for the stairs, but it transpired she just wanted to see what the elevator in a garage looked like. He did not mind the closed cubicle anyway, because she provided distraction – she dropped her newspaper, which fell into different sections, before dividing into swirling pages, and he had to pick them all up.

Out on the street, she headed away from home.

He caught her arm and asked, '*Xalti*, where are you going?'

'You said you wanted to go to a park.'

She directed him to an overgrown cobbled path that led steeply downhill towards the river. She didn't need his help – her sneakers were more suitable than his tie shoes for such expeditions. After they had covered some distance, they arrived at an elevated highway that runs parallel to the river, throwing a shadow below that discourages visitors. The park path leads beneath this overpass, and if you simply continue towards the river, you soon escape the shadow of the road and reach paradise. Few New Yorkers know of it, and those that do, want to stay – they bring their worldly possessions there, they pitch tents or build little huts with scrap metal in the underbrush, and they try to live happily ever after. They have no address there, they receive no mail, and rarely visitors. When two newcomers like Alan and his old neighbour appear there, they do not welcome them. They hide. The vegetation protects them from voyeurs, even in winter. The traffic roaring along the highway shields them acoustically. One can shout at the top of one's lungs there, and no one could ever overhear. This paradise is without conversation.

This did not prevent Mrs Allen from speaking as they walked further and further away from Broadway. When they finally reached the treeless banks of the Hudson, and the great feet of the Bridge, her conversation became audible to Alan.

'I prefer mountain scenery. Where I was born, there were

mountains. The Alps. There could be found a rare thing called silence.'

'I have heard of the Alps,' he said. He looked across the water, filled with dirty icebergs, to the grey cliffs on the far side of the river. 'Our mountains are taller.'

'The American mountains are much nicer,' she said sternly. 'I don't mean those here in New York, the Catskills, they are absolutely an embarrassment. But – listen, don't you consider yourself an American yet? You have every right to, you know. That is the best thing about this country. They're forever invoking God and their national superiority here, and sounding off in the most obnoxious, self-deluded way about democracy, but they have nothing against newcomers. Let's go to the red lighthouse.' She gestured to a small tower that stood beneath the huge bridge. 'Out in the West, the mountains are much more spectacular than anything in Turkey. It is my dream to see them. When I get my driver's licence, I will go there. Good riddance, New York.'

He did not hide his scepticism, and it stung her.

'You think I'm just – I don't know. Old. I know you think I'm old. Don't you!' she said. The word old cost her some courage.

'No, of course not,' he said.

'You're not so young yourself, you know,' she said. 'You'll see: a few more mornings, and you'll wake up in your seventies. But long before that, I'll have left New York. One of these days, I'll pass my driver's test. By noon, I'll own a car. Maybe one just like yours. By sundown, I'll be gone. And you and the bridge club will be on your own.'

He did not consider the possibility troubling.

'Be quiet, Xalti,' he said, and took her arm again.

She was heading eagerly towards the span overhead, the bridge. Its undersides were far up in the sky. Seen from below, the bridge had the power of a cathedral, making anyone bold enough to stand beneath it feel insignificant, a coincidence. The structure dwarfed the old red lighthouse that stood on an outcrop of rocks below.

'Once, the lighthouse served an important purpose. Now it has none. Scarcely anyone knows of its existence. It is a little like me.' She let go of his arm, stared upwards. She hummed a little under her breath, testing the echo. Her voice reverberated. She began to sing suddenly in a high-pitched quivering voice, *'Freude schoener Goetterfunken, Tochter von Elysium.'*

The melody was familiar. When he saw that she was safely posted, he turned his back to her, walked away, removing the gun from the back of his pants. At a distance from her, he took aim. He practised shooting her. Her singing was borne on an echo to him. He walked a little further away.

He heard his feet grinding on the snow, a squeak.

*   *   *

'Actually, you really must come to my club. I would like you to see it. And I'd like to see how you look in the right surroundings. I've always thought a killer would fit right in at the Sentinel Club. Do come, as a personal favour to me. It's the most exclusive club in New York. At least two members have to sponsor a candidate for membership, and then there is a heated debate about whether to take him or not. We reject 68 per cent of all those who make it into the final round. I can also show you the rugs I donated to the club — for the Reading Room. You'll appreciate them, all Kurds do.'

'Maybe another time.'

'Tell me, what do you do all night? You haven't been out once! You should go and see the red-light district. Then give me a call and I'll come and pick you up. We'll have a drink at the club. It's very close. Or do you need twelve hours of sleep a night!'

'Another time, thank you.'

He had been wondering whether to tell Mr Ballinger of his discovery, that Sulymon's wife was planning to leave him. But Alan decided to wait. He had to ask himself, why was he helping Sulymon Erkal feel sad, when he could actually be feeling ridiculed? By doing his job, Alan was denying himself a capital revenge.

Later that evening, he began feeling hungry and restless. He imagined returning to Broadway, to see Pat, who would be nice, or maybe another girl who would be even nicer, would would, when someone knocked on his door. He sidled to the door with his gun, and peered through the peephole: Mrs Allen. Alan tiptoed away from the door. But as he really had nothing better to do, he returned to the front door and opened it.

She addressed him as she was pushing through his doorway.

'I brought you a present.' The present was a new bottle of cheap California sherry, a tin of tuna fish and *The New York*

Times. 'I was too busy to finish the paper again today,' she complained, and proceeded into his kitchen.

Alan hastily hid the gun with the cutlery.

'Certain fish are high in unsaturated fat,' Mrs Allen said. 'One tin a day and one can extend one's longevity. Live long and carefully, I always say. Courage is a terrible vice. My husband was a soldier in the First World War. He had the luck to be sent to the Italian front. The Italians are sensible too. He was cornered by a group of Italian soldiers. They were quicker than he – they surrendered before he could. So he got a medal of honour. His mother was very angry with him. She thought he had been taking chances. Tuna fish tastes very well with sherry. Salt and the astringent taste of a first-class sherry. I brought all my openers. My tin-opener is probably older than I am. But just as reliable. I don't understand the new models.'

Alan opened the sherry, while she laboured over the tin. She splashed oil everywhere and still she couldn't get it open. Alan took over, finished the job. But he nicked his finger in the process.

Mrs Allen cried out, 'Oh dear. You are bleeding.' She looked away in consternation. 'I can't stand the sight of blood. It makes me terribly dizzy.'

She was standing up, leaning against the table, and now she stepped back, stumbled, veered and slowly swooned, right there in the kitchen, so that he was forced to catch her, hold her, and call, '*Xalti! Xalti*, wake up!'

She did not. Her condition worsened instantly. Her skin colour was white. Her eyes rolled open and did not see him.

Her jaw hung ajar, to the side, as if it had come unhinged. She had small, worn, grey teeth. Her tiny body turned heavy, as if all the years of her existence had been added to it. Her limbs dangled. And Alan's heart began pounding, completely out of control. The feeling that had dogged him all day came back in a rush and still he did not recognize it, he simply felt ill. Mrs Allen was dead. He really was on his own. And he would have to dispose of her body.

* * *

He carried her corpse into his living room, laid her down on his bed, removing her sneakers. He kissed her on her fluffy white hair, and on her forehead, and then he laid his head to her chest. His dejection grew. Cracks seemed to open everywhere in his calmness, and unhappiness began to trickle out. Trickle turned to torrent. Despair is a dangerous river. He gasped and clung to her. Finally, he wept.

After a while, the blue eyes opened and peered at him. 'I'm sorry if I frightened you,' she said.

His heart beat double time so that he gasped again, his relief somehow causing him another spasm of panic.

'*Allah sükür!*' he called, sitting up.

'Oh goddammit, stop that!' she replied.

Hastily, Alan held his injured finger out of sight.

'Let me get you the sherry,' he said.

He washed off the blood. The wound was minor, no longer bleeding. He spooned the fish on to paper plates, poured sherry into Styrofoam cups, and set the bedside table in the living room with sweeping hand gestures, like a first-class waiter, like a *kapüçe* looking for a tip.

They held up their glasses and both called, '*Noş!*'

Alan added, 'I mean it.'

Mrs Allen looked surprised and said, 'Don't worry about me. I intend to stick around for a while longer. Have you never seen anyone faint?'

'No.' He shook his head, still shocked.

'Well, there's always a first time for lots of things, even late in life. Today, you nearly experienced someone dying. Next thing, you'll fall in love. Then you really won't know what hit you. You'll think you've gone crazy.' She lay back on his pillow, and added, 'I hope I live to see that.'

'Did you love anyone besides your husband?' he asked, although it was not his habit to take any interest in the affairs of others.

'I never wanted to marry,' she said. 'But I was very difficult. I lived at home, and although I was already twenty-five years old, I was always fighting with my parents. So they decided to marry me off. They engaged a marriage broker. And he found Gustav, who was thirty and unmarried. I met him once, and agreed to marry him, just to get away from my family. And after about a year, we fell in love with each other. Then he started coming home from the university in the afternoon, just to visit me, and I still remember each of those visits in exact detail. I never loved another man, no. Why should I? But why do you ask? Are you married?'

'No, I swear that's not for me. But I'm not asking on my account. I was thinking about the woman we saw today. And her boyfriend. I think women are devils. What do you think?'

She answered coolly, 'Her husband is probably not satisfying her. Possibly he's a bad lover. Anyway, it's a romantic age now. People watch television, and aspire to true love. As a result, there's hardly such a thing as a happy marriage any more.'

Alan had an idea.

'I would like to see some television.'

'Well, why don't you go and get mine. I never watch it. Here are my keys.'

Alan returned with the little TV set, installed it in the living room, hurried back into the kitchen, for the chair and the sherry glasses, while she watched him from the cot and remarked, 'You are a strong man. The way you carry that chair! You will do well in America. But you'll have to stop smoking.'

Alan lit a cigarette and turned on the television, fiddling with the antenna until he got reception. A game show.

'Silly stuff,' Mrs Allen protested, but then she was amused. Bad picture quality didn't bother her.

Late at night, the cockroaches came out and feasted on the leftovers. They ignored the two people, one of them asleep in the bed, the other upright in a chair, a coat over his lap.

SIX

THE NEXT MORNING, THE city was dark and dank, with the sky slammed shut overhead. The taxi headed for the subject's block, Mrs Allen resting in the back, reading the newspaper with one eye, or talking too much. Lately she had been going on and on about trying one last time to get her own driver's licence. She wanted to drive once across the country. She wanted to see it as long as she was still healthy. She said this in a demanding way, without any self-pity. 'I need that driver's licence,' and then she added in English, 'Goddammit.' After she had used this expression several times in the course of several blocks, Alan asked her what it meant. She wouldn't tell him. She said it had God in it, and therefore it was rather pathetic that she was using it. But it was an expression of disgust.

He tried saying it, and this pleased Mrs Allen, so he kept saying it as he drove, shouting it, 'Goddammit!' which made him sound, stated Mrs Allen, like an authentic taxi driver. Whereupon he asked her, 'What makes you think I am not authentic!' as if he was offended. Before she could apologize, they reached their destination.

He parked across the street. From this vantage point, he could see that the house of Erkal was being rocked by drama. The smaller of the two Erkal children was crouching in front of the house, her head bent down. Her tears were silent but visible, as she shuddered from top to bottom, partly because she was suppressing the usual soundtrack. She stared at a small white heap. Alan approached, and saw that the object of the child's hysterical attention was a mouse, lying on its side. He turned away and smoked a cigarette. He heard the front door open again, and the footsteps of another child running down the stone steps. He caught a glimpse of her as she reached the sidewalk, tiny but energetic, her black braids under the control of a knitted cap. She was carrying a package which she set down in front of her sister, saying, in a stage whisper, 'Stop crying, everything has to die. Look, I've got a nice coffin. Mommy won't notice it's gone. This is the box she never touches. I found it in the back of her closet.'

She shook the paper bag and a box dropped into her hand. This was, judging by the heavy ornamentation and the shape, a jewellery box.

'Shut up!' she hissed as her sister began to cry again.

She opened the box, which proved to be brimming. She scooped out the shining contents, shoving them into the pockets of her snowsuit. Finally, she tipped the box and shook it vigorously. A ring tumbled out, rolling along the sidewalk. She gave chase. She caught it, and added that to her pocket too. She squatted down next to her sister, gingerly picked up the stiff dead mouse, and flung it unceremoniously into the box saying, 'How disgusting dead things are!'

She glared at her sister, whose tears began to drip again, and admonished her.

'Isn't it the loveliest coffin? Much nicer than Grandpa's was. Now stop crying and give me your hand.'

The smaller child obeyed the second command, not the first. The tears kept coming. Her big sister kissed her impatiently on the forehead, grabbed her hand and set off in the direction of the corner park, carrying the jewelled coffin in front of her stomach with appropriate solemnity. Alan slipped along behind them, watching. He saw the boys approaching from the far side of the park. From their cocky stride, and the way their heads turned this way and that, he knew they were not on their way to a mosque. One of them spotted the jewellery box, pointed at it. They all focused on the two little girls walking towards them. When they were abreast of each other, one of the boys held up a knife. Alan could see it gleam in the air. The boy spoke loudly, pointing the knife at the box. Another boy snapped open a knife too.

Alan hurried. But before he had gone more than a few feet, the girls had already handed over the jewellery box obediently and were doing what they had learned to do in the big city when confronted by bad men – run away. He watched them scampering into the park, while the boys hurtled in another direction, into a grove of trees. A short smug silence issuing from the grove ended with a blood-curdling shriek.

He saw the stiff dead mouse flying through the air. It rolled over and over before briefly reaching cruising altitude, and beginning its descent. Alan lost sight of it. He looked in the grove. The box lay in the snow. He picked it up and returned to the sidewalk where the two Erkal girls were just timidly exiting the park, even more dishevelled than usual. They were clearly looking for the mouse.

He strode up to them with the box.

'Girls,' he said in Turkish, 'bring the box back where you found it.'

The children gaped and accepted the box.

'Thanks, mister,' they said.

'Go home!' he commanded.

They looked at him, grabbed each other's hands, and ran. At once, he was infuriated with himself for speaking to the girls. That odd feeling had come upon him again now. He could not define it. He thought about it and decided it was some kind of 'narrowing' of his heart. That's what it felt like.

Driving upriver on Broadway, he was glad to have Mrs Allen sitting there behind him. She was a willing collaborator. She wanted nothing from him in return for her services. Perhaps she could be useful in other ways too. It occurred to him that he could be useful to her too. This selfless reflection was novel to our hero, and must be blamed on the circumstances: that he was a foreigner now. Living things accommodate in different ways to strange surroundings. Cats explore, ducks freeze, for hours and days on end, horses turn mean and jittery. After a while, familiarity settles in, but disorientation leaves a lasting impression: some become more energetic, some more lethargic, some become cruel. Alan was becoming more considerate. He thought about making some *gifkati* for Mrs Allen. The ceiling was low enough. She might enjoy it. He did not offer this to her, though. Instead he squired her to her door, and there, he shook her hand.

At this point, she said, 'Thank you.'

He responded by gazing at her for several seconds, not intending to affect her with the size and glitter of his eyes, but because he wanted her to understand that he was grateful to her. He might have just said, 'It is I who have to thank you!' but he couldn't. That was one of the many sentiments he felt embarrassed to say.

*   *   *

When he returned home, he heard a rustling in his kitchen. He entered, to find Mr Ballinger and his henchmen standing around, leafing through Mrs Allen's newspaper.

'Since when do you take an interest in the news?' Mr Ballinger called loudly.

Alan did not act surprised to see them there.

'Hello. Do you want a glass of sherry?' he asked.

But Mr Ballinger shook his head.

'No. You look tired. We're here to discuss some details of the job. Also your salary. Here.' He waved an aeroplane ticket. 'Look at this. You fly at 8.30 p.m. As Doug Turck. A name you can easily remember. You just have to learn to spell it.'

Dag Türkü, Mountain Turk. A fat insult for a Kurd. May

all the woes of Baghdad concentrate into a boulder and fall on his head.

Mr Ballinger put the ticket back in his jacket pocket.

'That's you after tomorrow, after you've finished the job. And here –' he removed another piece of paper, and flagged it – 'is a driver's licence made out to the same. Born in Ankara. And I also have your naturalization papers.' He put this away again. 'You'll fly to Miami. You'll like it. Nice and warm. Palm trees. The ocean.'

'I prefer the mountains. I hate water.'

'You don't have to go in it. We put you in my favorite neighbourhood. It's the scene. I hope you'll come to like it. Now I'm holding on to all this until tomorrow. I just want you to know it's all ready for you. Do your work punctually. A driver comes to pick up Sulymon Bey at 6 p.m. By six fifteen you are inside the house, by six thirty you are outside again. You drive straight to the airport, pick up these documents from a locker at Terminal 3. I'll give you the locker number when you've delivered the goods. Then you fly away. Our man will pick you up in Miami. He'll recognize you. You can discuss all your dreams for the future with him. You look a sight, incidentally. Professional killers go well dressed in America. But I like your moustache.'

He looked Alan over and remarked, 'You used to be such a natty dresser. *Canêmin*. There's a film of you, shows you working. Maybe you don't even know that. It's quite the classic. Has been circulating for several years. Just a short. You are fun to watch. So quick. Decisive. Without any sentimental hesitation. You had more hair then. And your forearms look so good in

116

a white shirt. Wear a white shirt tomorrow, please. Don't forget we need you to be punctual. We want those bodies to smell when he returns. Turn up the heat before you leave the house, please. I have choreographed everything for you. That's my real profession, I'm a choreographer! When the limo leaves, you enter the house. You can ring.'

Alan objected, 'At six fifteen, Tuerkan, the maid, will still be there.'

But he brushed that off.

'She doesn't matter.'

'Her husband will look for her.'

'Then wait till she leaves. When does she go?'

'At six thirty.'

'Then wait till six forty-five. Leave the taxi in front. Take care of them at once, no conversation, and it doesn't matter who goes first. Don't forget the ears. You've never killed children before. To my knowledge.'

Alan did not acknowledge this.

'When you're finished, close the door behind you. And drive slowly to the airport, taking the Fifty-Ninth bridge. You better check your map or you'll get lost. Park in Terminal 3, on the roof. Leave the gun and the ears in the car. Leave the key in the car and lock the door. Go down to the departure hall. I will have called you by the time you get there, and you'll know where to find your locker. Now I'll try your sherry.'

Alan fetched Mrs Allen's sherry. Mr Ballinger inspected the label and addressed the others.

'My God, is he trying to poison himself?!'

*   *   *

117

After Mr Ballinger and his merry band of *falan-filan* had left, Alan was glad he had not told him the truth about Sulymon Erkal's impending dilemma. He did not want to lose the job. He imagined the inconvenience of taking another one to earn his freedom. It was time to prepare himself for his day of hard work. The first thing he needed to work was clean hands, and a new hair colour. At his favourite store, he picked up a bottle of black hair dye.

He had spotted the other shop earlier, a store window with the outline of a hand and foot drawn on it, and a price list. Inside, were a row of thrones and chatting Chinese girls. His entrance seemed to please them very much – they surrounded him, murmuring like warm little waves. He nodded when he heard the word manicure, nodded again when he heard pedicure, and was led to a throne. His shoes were removed with solemnity, his feet settled into a tub that was filling up with steaming perfumed water, while a tray was set down before him, his hands laid into a bowl of the same special water.

He relaxed. What luck to be the only customer. What even greater luck to be the only man. Pampering and happiness are one. It transpired that the staff, like Alan, could not speak any English, not beyond a few essential words of their trade. One hears that the manicure business in New York is firmly in the hands of illegal immigrants, without green cards, and if you ask them, they will tell you that no, they do not have green cards, because they are 'international'. They attended to Alan's needs with exceptional care. His *Kir* made a spectacle of himself. Alan pulled his jacket closed over his lap but it was too late, the women had seen what was going on. They grew cold-hearted. They continued their work, but their grip on him became hard as manacles.

The ankle and wrist manacles had been left on when the police questioned him after his arrest. They had assumed he was a member of an outlawed Kurdish political party. He was not. Once, briefly, he had spent a few days assisting a childhood friend who belonged to a political group. They had a policy of two days of practicals, five days of theory. The practical was fun for a young man – bank robberies, detonating bombs – but the theory bored him. He preferred having a good car to having a state. One morning, when the insurgents were holed up in a southern town, the Turkish military moved in.

The mullah perching up on the minaret to call out the morning prayer saw the troops approaching. He included them in his prayers.

'*Allah u ekbar*. The wolves are coming from the west,' he sang in Kurdish. '*Allah Allah*. Every man for himself. Leave quietly, Don't forget your weapons.'

A soldier questioned the mullah about the sudden inclusion of Kurdish phrases in the Arabic chant, but the mullah explained that he had exhorted the locals to pray for a local woman suffering from a complicated pregnancy. Alan considered sneaking around a humiliation, and after this experience, he dropped out of the group, and subsequently avoided all political discussions.

When he was arrested many years later, the police tried to

wrest political information from him, by the usual means. They kept him in 'the bath', a tub filled to the brim with faeces, giving him nothing to drink but a wet rag to suck. When he lost consciousness after three days, they pulled him out, fed him thick tea that hiked his adrenalin level, making him tremble and twitch, as if he was deathly afraid. Later, they concentrated on his *Kir*, who was a sensitive sissy. They didn't know about his vanity, so they did something wrong, and Alan proved strangely indifferent.

Asked to name his terrorist group, he volunteered, 'One Kurd is too few, two Kurds are too many.' Thereafter he lapsed into silence.

He impressed his tormentors by not screaming or babbling or shedding a tear. He existed, with extreme pain or without it – he showed no fear because he felt no fear, not even of electrical devices. For the time being, they laid aside their tools. There was plenty of time to demonstrate their art later, after his conviction, when they would have years alone with him. The pressure on his hands and feet let up. The girls were finished.

He looked around him in bewilderment.

'Galegale,' said one curtly. Her English was rotten. As he did not respond, she grabbed a piece of paper and wrote on it, '$40.' She shoved this unceremoniously into the very hand she had serviced.

His memories had ruined his first taste of luxury in the New World. At least, he now felt prepared for the job. His finger on the trigger would be a pleasure to behold.

*   *   *

At midnight, he lay smoking on his cot, leafing through his English grammar book with little interest. After he had learned that the Kurdish word *şad* meant happy in English, and having tried without much success to figure out the pronunciation of an h, he flung the book aside and devoted himself to laziness. He should be thinking through the chores he planned for the next day. Instead, he day-dreamed. By and by, he imagined showing his grandmother around his apartment in Istanbul. The necklace of heavy gold medallions he wished he had given her blazed on her black dress. Her face was vague to him; he could not picture it. In fact, he could not really remember it. He watched her enter the kitchen, stare at the microwave and ask, 'Is this a television?' He demonstrated the powers of this amazing invention, while she shook her head, smiling at him proudly.

He had received the news of her death two years after it happened, when he bumped into the old grocer from his home town on the street. The merchant had recognized his fellow villager waiting at a red light, although Alan was dressed in the yellow togs of an electrician, for a job in an office building. His *simbêlpîj* had probably given him away. The grocer had also informed Alan that their town no longer existed. He himself had moved to Diyarbakir, and when the war followed him there, to Istanbul. His granddaughter was with him, propping him up, and asked Alan shrilly why he wasn't in the mountains, with the organization. Her brothers and sisters were all fighting. She had been forced to stay behind to look after the very young and the very old in the family. Her father was in jail for singing a Kurdish song in the street. He had been drunk. 'But your grandmother died in her bed, before your house was burned down,' the old grocer assured him. The phone rang. Alan looked at the offending object and finished his cigarette before answering.

'Would you like to join me at my club?' asked Mr Ballinger.

He did not.

But Mr Ballinger said, 'I have something for you here,' and Alan hoped this might be a better weapon, that the Smith and Wesson had just been Mr Ballinger's idea of a joke. So he agreed to drive downtown to the Sentinel Club.

'Please wear a jacket and tie,' Mr Ballinger added.

But our hero no longer possessed a tie! Self-pity wracked him.

'And take the subway. You won't find a place to park around here. Here's how you get here –'

After listening to Mr Ballinger's instructions, Alan shook out the trousers he had now worn for nearly a week, and with each shake he wondered what was in store that evening. He smoothed down his hair, and with each pat, he scrutinized that emptiness called the foreseeable future. Then he smoothed down his eyebrows, and decided to drive anyway. He would find a parking space. *Hila hila*, he did so. He felt victorious, the city could not vanquish him. The inhabitants fled, hid in their houses – the streets were deserted when he reached the large solemn building that housed the club. There was a turmoil inside, though. Mr Ballinger was waiting in the lobby, one of a crowd of expensive suits and dresses.

Mr Ballinger gave him a cold welcome.

'You can't come here like that. I told you to wear a tie!' He studied Alan, watching anger move across his face in a quick, violent storm. He smiled into the danger and apologized. 'Of course. I'm so sorry. You have no tie, do you. You absolutely must buy yourself some clothes when you've finished the job. But here. I have a starting-out present for you –' He handed him a splendid gold tie. 'Something fit for a Kurdish king.' Alan donned it gladly. 'But you better give me your mobile phone, it's not allowed in here. Papers and books aren't allowed either. Special rules of conduct. People don't want to be disturbed here. Clubs are a dying luxury. The fitness studios have replaced them. And oh, your cigarettes. No smoking here.'

He checked in these items at a desk and led Alan up a spacious set of stairs. Portraits hung everywhere.

'Famous club members that are no longer with us,' said Mr Ballinger sadly.

Alan didn't pay attention – he was wondering how he could get his cigarettes back.

'And now let me point out some of the living ones to you. Over there is the state senator from this district, and a couple of his business friends. That's a famous writer. You have to get elected. There are my friends, they've found a table!'

They were just sitting down in the corner of a wood-panelled dining room. He introduced Alan.

'Doug Turk, nicknamed the Black Stone. A famous actor from Istanbul. Who really should become a member some day, after he has made his debut in this country. He doesn't speak any English yet. So you can admire his looks.'

Vague interest flickered in some eyes, competitiveness in others. As they sat down at the end of the table, Alan caught chitchat about Istanbul. For a while, the company compared notes on their visits there. It seemed everyone had been there at least once and could knowledgeably discuss some excellent restaurants.

Mr Ballinger asked his guest what he would like to drink. 'Whisky,' said Alan. 'And give me my cigarettes.'

Mr Ballinger sighed, and looked troubled.

'Can you control yourself for a while?' he asked. 'I'll get you a dozen whiskys if you promise not to talk to me about smoking. Your smoking is very embarrassing. What did you do on the plane, anyway?'

He ordered one whisky, remarking, 'Actually, most people drink wine here, not hard stuff.'

Alan stared at him, detecting the frilly undergarments of his face that made it flare at the cheeks, and droop slightly at the chin. Mr Ballinger turned away abruptly, and called to a friend across the table. This freed Alan, allowing him to notice his other neighbour, a dark-haired beauty hiding her charms – her full hips – with a masculine off-the-rack jacket. Her pants wrapped her thighs tightly, as if they were a pair of hot, aromatic sausages. She must have been an American by the sounds of her but when the Italian waiter appeared with his pad, she insisted on speaking Italian to him. The waiter replied steadfastly in English.

'*Con pomodore!*' she said, trilling the r's.

'Do you mean with tomatoes?' he asked.

She spoke about an opera she had seen in Rome, which she pronounced Rrroma.

By now, the conversation was in full swing.

Mr Ballinger leaned over towards Alan, and said, 'We are discussing spices. Sharp spices offer protection against certain cancers. Do you like them too?'

Alan conceded it.

Mr Ballinger looked pleased.

'Sharp spices cauterize the asshole. I always eat them for dinner. I look forward to the sensation of burning the next morning. I remember in Kurdistan, the men took towels to the toilet to dry their tears. The screams of men defecating woke up the village long before the cock crowed.'

Mr Ballinger was right, but Alan was angry. A cigarette! In the plane, he had smoked in the bathroom, into the sink, with the water running, and the drain pumping, creating wind suction that siphoned off the smoke. He had spent his last *preservatif* to cover the smoke detector. But the club took sterner precautions, and Alan was stranded. He calmed himself by fantasizing about brutal sex with his neighbour. She did not notice. She was enraptured by something else, which astonished him – the conversation.

Periodically, Mr Ballinger translated.

'We are discussing Bosnia,' he said.

Alan's neighbour sat up straight: she became weighty as a statue on a square. The difference is, she wanted to speak. Finally, she did, pitching her words forwards. Alan kept hearing 'Aj', 'Aj', with a slight pause before and after, so that it was clearly a word of unusual importance. The others interrupted the beauty. They too used the word 'Aj' in that remarkable fashion.

'We are arguing about the Middle East,' Mr Ballinger informed him. And later, 'We are talking about the stock market.'

This discussion was interrupted by a hubbub. The kitchen, said the waiter, pointing at his watch, was closed. The guests could only order dessert. Cries of disappointment. Anger. The waiter took them calmly. He waved his arm, and a dessert cart was wheeled to the table. The attractions there silenced complaints.

The dark-haired beauty pointed to the raspberries and trilled, '*Frrrragoli, prrrego.*'

The waiter looked angry.

'The Italian word for raspberries,' he said, 'is *lamponi*, madam.' He laughed in a nasty way, but the others did not.

The company looked down at their plates, obviously embarrassed. The beauty grew pale, and remarked something about her eyesight, she had thought they were strawberries, from a distance, etc. The cart had come to Alan, who pointed at several confections, and said in English, 'And, and, and,' to indicate that he wanted all of them. The other diners stared at him tensely, envious of his lack of inhibitions, and also concerned that at the end of the evening the bill would be divided evenly among them, in which case they would have to underwrite this man's appetite.

The dessert came, suppressing conversation. When pleasure had ended, talk began again. His neighbour initiated it. She was enraged about something.

'A magazine article,' explained Mr Ballinger, for Alan's edification, 'has just been published, with a proposal to close the state prisons. Instead, criminals will be sentenced to a variable number of evenings at the opera.'

As she spoke, the beauty's black hair swung in the draught of her great emotion, her hands darted, her gaze was glazed by passion, she swayed at the table. Her thigh kept rubbing Alan's thigh.

'The conviction for a traffic offence,' said Mr Ballinger in one of Alan's ears, 'might carry a sentence of one visit to the local opera house. Involuntary manslaughter would be punished by two or three visits, arson and first-degree murder with up to ten visits to the Metropolitan opera – more would be cruel and unusual punishment.'

The beauty's thigh was now pressed hard against Alan's thigh.

'The opera would prove a great deterrence to crime, and it was cost-efficient because one evening imprisoned in a contemporary opera production takes as much time subjectively as ten years in a prison cell. Even someone committing a crime of passion, his hand raised to do the bloody deed, would meekly lower his hand again, if he knew what awaited him.'

The beauty cried out something, her thigh was on its own again.

'She says the magazine should never have published such an article, because it undermines the already endangered

127

institution. She also points out that the author's husband is a lawyer who defends Communists.'

The beauty had stirred up a hornet's nest of talk, and now settled back into her chair with that proud look of right-eousness satisfied. Her thigh returned to its moorings, against Alan's thigh.

Mr Ballinger became too involved in the ensuing debate to translate for Alan, so our hero had nothing to do but listen to the strange syllables being exchanged around him. Throughout this time, his neighbour's thigh remained pressed tightly again his, with just two layers of thin fabric separating them. After some time had passed, he felt it would be polite to reciprocate. He rubbed his thigh back and forth, taking command of the impending seduction. Then he laid his hand under the table, and settled it gently on her knee. This was round and warm and quaked like a bunny.

Abruptly, she yanked her entire leg away. She turned sideways, towards him. Her eyes opened fire, while her open hand pounded his leg. She was very strong, and her blows hurt. At the same time she blared something to the other diners that caused them all to turn their heads and smile at him condescendingly.

Mr Ballinger taunted him.

'They think you are behaving like a typical Arab.'

This stung Alan, and he said, 'Tell her she is beautiful.'

But this apparently antagonized Mr Ballinger, who snapped, 'You have no idea how offensive you are being.' He seemed to be apologizing for his guest. A certain calm returned.

After a while, the event was forgotten by all but the beauty, who kept her chair a few inches away, and kept shooting him infuriated looks. His day-dreams dried up. Torment began: he wanted a smoke. But a heavenly force was on Alan's side, and sent rescue. A big fat cockroach, probably all the way up from Alan's neighbourhood, came swaggering slowly across the table. Nobody else noticed it, and it promenaded around the dishes for a while. Finally, Alan turned to his neighbour, said, 'Hm, hm,' nodding towards the insect.

The hue and cry that followed dispersed the company so quickly that no one thought of paying. Mr Ballinger was left with the bill.

As they waited for change, Mr Ballinger remarked bitterly to him, 'Now you'll tell everybody there are cockroaches at the Sentinel Club.'

*   *   *

Perhaps Mr Ballinger was angry about the large bill he had been forced to pay, or embarrassed about the cockroach. His face grew gloomy. After retrieving their telephones and cigarettes from the concierge, he insisted on walking Alan to his taxi, and then he got in the front seat, and rode with him wordlessly, staring straight ahead at the road, all the way back up Broadway. Alan parked in the garage and still Mr Ballinger made no effort to say goodbye. He followed Alan up the stairs, into the building, up the next stairs, to his apartment. He came inside.

Alan went directly into the kitchen, sat down, folded his hands on the table and said, 'What can I do for you?'

'I'm sending you back to Turkey,' replied Mr Ballinger, standing in the doorway.

'Fine,' replied Alan.

Mr Ballinger grabbed his phone and dialled a number. Galegale. Then he leaned against the wall and waited. After a few minutes, the front door opened, and the janitor came in, his face and orange uniform looking rumpled. He laughed nervously.

'You're here to witness an interrogation,' Mr Ballinger said once in English and then again in Kurdish. He turned his attention to Alan, his voice matter of fact. 'Give us your real name.'

'Alan Korkunc.'

'It is not.'

'It is the name you gave me.'

'What is your real name!' snarled Mr Ballinger.

'Alan Korkunc,' replied out hero steadfastly. 'A name is something usually given to someone who is not asking for it. It doesn't last long. Because after a while, everyone gets the same name – they are all called dead. You and I will share that name sooner or later.'

The interrogator stared, his eyes suddenly amused, even affectionate.

'Well, you are certainly talkative now. So, tell me, what have you been doing with the neighbour?'

'The neighbour? I was helping her out.'

'You have never helped anyone out in your life. And how do you feel about being sent back to Turkey?'

'The flight to Istanbul leaves in the afternoon, so I will be sent tomorrow. As long as I am still here, I am not there. When I'm there, I'll know how I feel. I don't expect I'll feel much. They will kill me. As long as they haven't killed me, I'm still alive. And once they have killed me, I won't know that I am dead. The transition is scarcely worth mentioning.'

Mr Ballinger turned to the janitor and evidently ordered him to do something he didn't want to do, because the creature threw up his hands and shook his head in protest. Finally Mr Ballinger pointed at the door, and snarled at the janitor, who lowered his hands and, mumbling syllables, disappeared.

When the door had closed behind him, Mr Ballinger turned back to Alan and said, 'You can't even pay someone to be reliable these days. Stand up from there, and come over here.'

Alan advanced, his face expressionless.

Mr Ballinger removed a Beretta from his jacket and pressed it against Alan's forehead.

'Goodbye, asshole,' he said.

Alan's first, and his only, thought was his face: his face was going to be destroyed. His own beloved face. His pride deserted him – this was a practical matter.

'Not in the face,' he cried. 'In the heart. Here. Here. Or let me jump out of the window. In the other room. The drop is far enough. Bring me over there, I'll jump. But don't shoot, don't shoot.'

His begging seemed in his own ears to go on and on, while the feeling of tightness in his heart grew ever more violent, until his limbs began to shake with it. Then, finally, he was able to identify that feeling: fear. Mr Ballinger snickered and pulled the trigger.

The evening had ended badly. Alan lay sprawled on the kitchen floor. His trousers were soaking because he had soiled himself, and his body was stiff. He had been lying in the same position for hours. Finally, he managed to move his hands to his face. He felt the features: nose, eyes, mouth. All were still in their familiar places. Nothing had changed. His forehead was dry and intact. He stood up. His legs had no difficulty resuming their duties: they carried him to the cot. He dropped his coat as he went and his trousers on the floor and lay down, pulling the blanket around him. He wallowed in comfort. But embarrassment, with its thousand fingers, poked at him, picked at him, and unravelled the joy he felt at having survived. He had been afraid. And Mr Ballinger's gun had been unloaded.

*   *   *

Time is a strong soap, but it is can't clean a man's memory of humiliation, nor trousers of a bad soiling. The next morning, Alan washed his pants and put them on dripping wet. The intensity of embarrassment rises exponentially when there are witnesses to it, because reminder is a multiplying factor. The only way to rid oneself of this damn spot is either not to notice it, some are capable of this, or murder all those who remember it – embarrassment is greatly underestimated by historians as a triggering factor in world politics. Alan's ability to annihilate surged after last night's events; he became more dangerous, or perhaps less so – he became unstable.

He sought distraction. He shaved, and took aim at his *simbêlniviṣt*, sawing off the sides. Now the moustache lay in two short bars on his upper lip. A *simbêlzeytûnî*. With his trousers clinging to his body, as if he had just submerged his lower half in water, he knocked at his neighbour's door. He found her dressed to go out, and having, once again, a 'very bad mood'. She planned to take her driving test one last time. But she claimed they would fail her on account of her age.

'They take one look at me, and it's all decided,' she said. 'White hair. No licence.'

'I have an idea,' promised Alan, and left again.

He returned with a solution. He made her sit down, and placed two sardine tins on the floor at her feet, and a box of crackers in front of her on the table. He got down on his hands and knees – he was kneeling before her! – and placed her right foot, in its black pump, on the left-hand tin.

'Those are your breaks,' he told her. He straightened up, and laid her hands on the cracker box. 'Your steering wheel. You have to practice.' He handed her his key. 'Start the car. Your gear shift is behind the wheel.'

'Now back out of your parking spot. But don't forget to check your mirrors.' As she played this game, he was wetting down her hair with a towel. 'Now you hold still,' he commanded. He set to work dying her hair black, while she practiced steering a car. He made car noises for her, 'Vroom vroom', and some screeching, which they both enjoyed. There was even enough hair colour for his own hair, or better said, there were few enough hairs on his head, and a drop of hair dye sufficed to cover them. The papers on the table were strafed with black.

Like a practised hairdresser, Alan rinsed Mrs Allen's head in the kitchen sink, made her sit down again, combed her hair. The thin hair dried quickly.

She spent a long time regarding herself in the bathroom mirror, and declared, 'I look like a young brunette now. They have to pass me. You know, in America you are only a free man if you have a driver's licence. I must hurry,' she said. 'When I come back, we'll celebrate.'

She put on her overcoat, but left the tea cosy on the pot. As an afterthought, she went to the nightstand and picked up the photo propped there, showing a little boy and his father. She slipped this into her coat pocket.

'If this brings luck,' she said, 'then I'll see my son again.'

Alan returned to his own apartment. He spent the remains of the afternoon chafing, smoking, sipping sherry, and practising with his gun. His trousers dried on his body. Whenever he heard movement on the landing, he rushed to the door. But it was just a series of neighbours. Finally, he heard slow faltering footsteps and he knew it was she. Mrs Allen was unlocking her own door, her expression crestfallen. She did not want to talk to Alan. When he said, 'Hello!' she just shook her head sadly.

Alan said ferociously, in English, 'I kill him.'

But Mrs Allen shook her head.

'No, no, I already nearly killed him. There was a red light. I just didn't notice it.'

*　　*　　*

When Alan cleaned up his 'home' for the last time, he remembered the television. He lugged it to his neighbour's apartment. He set the television down in its former place, and plugged it in.

Then he turned to the old woman and said simply, 'Xalti, goodbye.'

'Where are you going?' asked Mrs Allen, perturbed.

He thought about it.

'On an aeroplane.'

'But where?' she asked in consternation.

'Maybe Miami,' he said.

'It's hot there,' replied Mrs Allen. 'I prefer to be way above sea level.'

She was about to open a new bottle of sherry but Alan stopped her.

'Xalti, I have to go.' He glanced around the room, one last time, and saw that she had returned the photo to its accustomed place. Somehow, the importance of this photo irritated him.

'Don't you have any other photos?' he asked her. 'Maybe I should give you one of me.'

She shook her head.

'Oh, I don't need photos. You don't have photos either, do you? I lost mine a long time ago, when we went to Istanbul. There's really no danger that I will ever forget what my family looked like. I think of them much too often to forget them. My parents, my grandparents, my two older brothers, their wives, their children, my sister, my sister's fiancé. And all my friends. I remember them all, the way they looked. The way they smelled. I was the one who left. When will you be back?'

Alan shrugged. Then he hugged the old woman and kissed her eyelids.

'I've noticed,' she said, 'that you are wearing a moustache like Adolf Hitler's. I don't really like it.'

*　　*　　*

He was sweating profusely, partly because the weather had changed – spring was paying a short visit. The temperature had climbed into the 60s and the sun shone victoriously. He opened the windows and headed for the bathroom. As he undressed, he could hear Mrs Allen, one bathroom over, showering, singing 'Ode to Joy'. He slammed his window shut again. He did not wish to think about her. He had decided to get the job over with as quickly as possible. Just go in and take care of them, and hurry away. He wouldn't take the time to look over the kitchen gadgets, as he had planned. He was feeling unenthusiastic. He tried to wind himself up by showering and shaving again. The moustache was definitely handsome, although rather grey, which looked odd when the hair on his head was so black. He really had wasted his hair colour on Mrs Allen. Only to have her remark disparagingly about his moustache. Finally, he shaved it off altogether. He even removed the sideburns. For the first time in decades, he was really clean-shaven, like a youngster. Like any American man.

His taxi waited for him, not recognizing the importance of this, his last working day. Alan rolled down the windows. When he turned on the ignition, the meter resumed its slow climb. It was already in the high hundreds. Alan patted the passenger seat: he was through with this vehicle. He wouldn't miss it. He adjusted the rear-view mirror. Mrs Allen's image occupied most of it. She was sitting there, smiling her old head off.

'I thought I might accompany you to the airport. I am taking the day off from work today anyway. I will take the airport bus back.'

Alan was enraged. He did not want any distraction.

He shouted, 'No. No. No.' He yanked open the back door, and beckoned the old woman out, out, out. When she resisted, her face collapsing under all the woes of Baghdad, he pulled at the sleeve of that ridiculous coat, repeating, 'No! Understand? No.'

In retrospect, this scene is so unpleasant that I would like to shorten it. End it right there. Let's move on.

*　　*　　*

Late in the afternoon, Alan arrived at his job, all ready to start work. He parked directly across the street. The children came from school, fidgeting and quarrelling in front of the house. Tuerkan's scolding was shriller than usual, but more efficient. She got them indoors quickly. Their mother was nowhere to be seen. Then he caught sight of their father. Sulymon Erkal was standing in the window, staring at the strangely warm weather. He was dressed in a sombre suit, and held a prayer book in his fat hand. His wife came up next to him, without touching him, her face expressionless, and looked out too. They didn't speak. Ajda Erkal opened the window. She wore a bright-blue blouse, something for the spring, for a new beginning. It had a round girlish collar.

Alan could make out chanting. They had the radio or television tuned to an Islamic mass.

Then Alan heard, 'Actually, people who can believe in God are very lucky.'

He shrugged at his passenger. He had not been able to get rid of Mrs Allen, and now she was making admissions in the back seat that did not interest him.

She went on, 'Unfortunately, I do not have that luck.'

A pizza delivery van pulled up. Tuerkan paid the delivery man in the doorway. The couple left the living-room window. The sermon ended in mid-sentence. The house was silent.

At five forty-five, a limousine arrived, idling at the kerb. At six o'clock, the chauffeur went to the door, and returned with a suitcase. Sulymon Erkal followed with an umbrella. His wife stood in the doorway and waved cheerfully as he climbed into the car. After the limousine had disappeared from view, Alan turned to his old passenger.

'We have to wait, and then I have to run inside for a few minutes. You stay here. Wait, OK? You have your books.' She had brought a dozen books, and her manuscript, as if she intended to stay a while. The back seat was covered with paper.

At six fifteen Tuerkan left the house, scurrying, not even giving a second glance to the taxi. In the back seat, Mrs Allen squinted at the newspaper. Just as Alan was getting ready to leave the car, a freshly polished red sports car arrived and double-parked directly in front of the door. Dave swaggered out. Alan watched with disgust as Dave trotted fearlessly up the stairs. He opened the front door with his own key. It occurred to Alan that Fortune was blessing his enterprise. He would have one more victim. This way, Sulymon Erkal would have an inkling of what his wife was up to. The assassin got out of the car, with more enthusiasm now. He forgot the telephone in the front seat.

The old woman still held the book to her eyes, but her head had fallen back on the seat, and she was clearly asleep, another bit of good luck. Alan entered the gate, and headed for the back entrance. The back door was still broken. The kitchen was dark; no one was inside. He entered.

*   *   *

The first thing he did was pull the shades in the kitchen, in case someone thought of running there, turning on the lights and making a hullabaloo. He spotted the paring knife he needed, and the rubber gloves beneath the sink, leaving them there for the moment. The dining room was dark, the living room well lit. He moved without trying to be quiet through the hallway, to the stairwell, and then took the stairs at a leisurely pace. The Smith and Wesson was dry and steady in his hand, a magic wand.

At the top of the landing, he could look directly into the children's room at his left, and the Erkal bedroom straight ahead. He wasn't expected, and no one heard him arrive. He could see the children lying on the floor on their stomachs. He could not help but take an interest in what they were watching – a naked couple were writhing on a bed. The man was tying the woman's hands to the bedpost. He caressed her neck, and kissed it. His long bare back formed an arch, and then straightened out again. He repeated this movement several times. The woman's eyes were closed, and she moaned. The children giggled loudly. Alan was stunned. Dave's voice revived him. He could see Ajda Erkal sitting at her dressing table, sideways to the hall. She was peering into a mirror and applying eye make-up. Dave was evidently standing just behind her because suddenly his white hands came into view on the front of her torso. She ignored them, as they fumbled their way inside the blue blouse and wandered beneath it. Alan guessed what he was saying, because the tone was whining and eager. Something like, 'I've never had you here, have I, darling. It doesn't seem fair.'

Alan watched in disgusted fascination. Indecision hung in a dead weight on his intentions. He couldn't decide which party he should kill first. The gun grew heavier in his hand. The children's rumps rocked with laughter. On the television screen in front of them, the woman had stopped moaning. She stared balefully at the viewer. A pair of men's hands were pressing on her neck. She looked frightened. In the master bedroom, Dave's hands had proceeded downwards, forcing themselves beneath the waistline of Ajda's skirt. He spoke urgently into her ear. She had put down her make-up, leaned backwards, her eyes closed. Alan looked from one room to the next, from one image to the next, his gaze switching back and forth, faster and faster. But another sound jarred him, sending him into even greater indecision – he heard the door open downstairs, heavy footsteps, and panting.

He glanced over the balustrade and saw the top of Sulymon Erkal's head, his ears dangling below.

Sulymon Erkal could not have seen Alan, but he felt his presence there, on the landing, and he called, 'Hello, you!'

*   *   *

The next few minutes, so eventful in Alan's life, passed with the leisurely pace common to catastrophe. From his position at the top of the stairs, Alan saw Ajda Erkal freeze into position, one hand at her eyebrow. Slight movement from Dave, as he slid away backwards, his hands extricating themselves from woman's clothing. The children slammed their door shut, and one could hear the television channels being switched, and the *Sesame Street* song sounded. Alan stayed where he was, his gun still steady.

Sulymon called loudly into the ensuing silence, 'I know there's another man here. I knew there would be when I left. I just knew it. I had to see for myself. He should have some courage, and come down to me. I want to talk to him.'

Still no movement from the master bedroom. Finally, Alan responded. He moved over to the stairs and looked down at Sulymon Erkal, into those hated brown eyes, into those little plates heaped with misery. Around them, Sulymon's face turned into a wrinkled, splotched tablecloth. Whimpering sounds issued from his throat.

He cried in Turkish, 'So it is really true. I'd hoped it wasn't. I'd hoped my suspicions were unfounded. I needed to know. This is a disaster. I wish I were dead.' He slumped against the wall, placed his hands over his face, and wailed like an old grandmother.

Meanwhile, Ajda Erkal had been activated. She came out of her room to the stairs, where she saw Alan, and began a

141

loud siren of a scream. She looked down at Sulymon and her screams took on form, became syllables: *'Polis! Polis!'*

At this point Sulymon Erkal hauled a gun out of his coat pocket, not just a gun – a 32 Walther – and aimed it upwards, at his wife. Alan moved slowly, as if he was wading through a swamp, towards Sulymon, who was trying to pull the trigger, but excitement made him fumble. As he advanced, Alan switched the Smith and Wesson into his left hand. With his right, he caught Sulymon's arm, and wrapped it around the owner's back, pinching the hand until it released the Walther into his own hand. *Hila hila*, that was better. He dropped the Smith and Wesson on to the floor. It fell silently into the plush carpet.

He swung the elderly paunchy man around, held him in front, pulling him along while he backed out, towards the open front door. He had reached the doorway, was standing backwards there, facing Ajda, clutching her husband. Finally he brought the loaded Walther to Sulymon's Byzantine ear. He saw the net of wrinkles on the lobe, the hair matted inside the passageway that led to the man's brain. An old helpless man. A split second of pity can wreck the best-made plans. But the assassin no longer had any plans. He simply wanted an end to the drama.

*   *   *

Meanwhile in the taxi, Alan's telephone began to ring, shaking Mrs Allen awake. She was confused. After a while, she localized the ringing noise in the front seat. She reached over, picked up the phone and regarded it. She had never seen such a phone. She did not know how to silence the ring. Finally, she tried pressing the green flashing button. She held the phone to her ear without saying anything. Then she heard a voice she had not heard in many years. She recognized it, of course. The voice said, 'Hello? Hello?' angrily, several times over. She pulled herself together. She had waited so many years for this moment, now it had come, and she was unprepared.

She said, '*Ez Ingilizi nuezanum.*'

Whereupon the voice demanded in Kurdish to speak to Alan Korkunc, Alan Korkunc, at once!

Her conviction satisfied, she said, in English, 'You don't even recognize the voice of your own mother?'

The caller hung up abruptly.

Mrs Allen got out of the car, her hands shaking for the first time, but not from old age. She proceeded towards the staircase, she sped up the stone stairs. Alan was standing with his back to her in the open front door.

She came right up to him and screamed in his ear, 'My son! You know my son! He has just called you on the phone!'

The noise startled Alan, who teetered forwards, pushing his hostage. Mrs Allen thought Alan was moving away from her. She grabbed him and pulled mightily, her unhappiness turned into pure energy – she yanked at Alan from behind so fiercely that he lost his balance altogether and began a slow, horrible tumble backwards down the stone stairway.

He thought he heard distant police sirens as he fell. He managed to drag himself to the street. His face and chest were dripping wet, so that he wondered how he had dirtied himself this time, and worried about the stains. The passenger seat of the taxi was open, where Mrs Allen had exited a few minutes earlier, and he dropped inside, expecting to find the old woman there. But she was not. She was sitting down behind the wheel.

'Close the door!' she snapped. She turned the ignition and began to drive. 'I'm not going to look at you. You're bleeding all over the damn place,' she said.

She drove nicely. He fell asleep. When he awoke, she was heading north on Broadway, probably towards home.

She was whizzing through traffic.

He came to his senses and asked her, 'Why the hell did you have to do that?'

And she replied, 'It's high time you learned English.'

Then she asked, 'Who calls you on that phone?'

He didn't understand her interest and he felt sick.

'Mr Ballinger, he replied. 'A horrible man. Who hired me to kill someone. But I didn't.' He added, 'I have no desire to kill anyone. It is a terrible profession. The pay is lousy, when you think about it.'

'Hired you to kill someone? You must be joking of course.'

'I am joking of course,' said Alan, and dozed for a while, until the phone rang again. He woke up then. 'Don't answer it!' he shouted. He grabbed the phone from the front seat, dropped it on the floor, and began to stamp on it. The phone came apart after a few blows, and he saw the bug that had been placed with the batteries. 'Pull over for a minute,' he ordered. She did, braking gently. He opened the window and tossed the phone into a corner trash bin. 'Can we find a highway?' he asked.

*   *   *

The taxi was travelling on the highway, in a rural area. An apple core flew out of the window. Then a cigarette stub. Then a Walther.

*   *   *

The meter had crested at several thousand dollars and no longer budged. Alan was driving again. Mrs Allen had a huge map of the United States spread on her lap. She turned on the radio and heard the following news bulletin: 'A murder attempt was allegedly made today on the family of a Turkish businessman living in New York. A Kurdish Terrorist Agency phoning Reuters to claim responsibility cited that the businessman's wife and two children had been slain in cold blood to teach him a lesson. The phone caller also alerted the police to the crime. The police were hastily dispatched, but reported only a domestic drama taking place when they arrived at the scene. However, a loaded firearm was confiscated on the property which was registered in the name of a family friend. This is under investigation.'

*   *   *

The assassin had been set up, led to a trap, and asked to step in. But he wasn't particularly ashamed, because he had escaped it, and chances were good he had embarrassed others in the process. These two tourists weren't going to think about their past any more. They looked at the country. Mrs Allen had never been. After they had crossed the Middle West and reached the mountains, they began to feel more and more comfortable. On the outskirts of Denver, they picked up a hitchhiker, a student who had just dropped out of college. She wanted to return home, to Tonopah, in the middle of Nevada, and attend to things that mattered, like her father's sheep and cattle ranch. They said they might as well take her there. When they reached Tonopah, Alan and Mrs Allen felt at home, too. Alan said it was just like Kurdistan, Mrs Allen said it was exactly like the Alps, the snow very deep, the peaks very high, the summers said to be cool and breezy.

The girl's father had a large guest house on his property, and he invited them to stay. Mrs Allen tried to buy a typewriter but there were none for sale in the entire state. Finally she bought a used computer at a garage sale and tried to learn how to use it. Alan proved himself just as unable to figure it out, which soothed her fear that she was too old to learn this new trick. Finally she gave up, and just read all day long, declaring herself entitled to a bit of laziness. Alan went to work at the local grocery store. They lived quietly, complacently, closely, the way they had in New York, except that they had a fair number of visitors and friends who dropped over and wanted to hear tales from far away – Americans are like that, they are curious people. After a while, English came to Alan. He welcomed it. He often found himself in the company of the college girl, and he wanted to talk to her. He had never known anyone like her, because he had never really known any girl at all. She was clever, she occasionally read books, she spent hours asking Mrs Allen about the past in Europe, and she loved her work at the ranch. She was patient with the newcomers, but she wouldn't let any man push her around, not for a minute. Nor could he touch her or even ogle her, not until she had known him for a long time.

By then, Mrs Allen had set Alan up with his very own gasoline station, and he was speaking English with ease. He began reading the newspapers he sold at the gas station, and took an interest in his surroundings. He read with increasing gusto, and even browsed the Bible, out of curiosity. He had no complaints. But he did. There was one hitch. Somehow, he was always waiting for this girl to appear. He felt any time spent without her was, it's hard to explain – wasted time. He became moody when she wasn't around, and exhilarated when she was, and Mrs Allen, who knew better, laughed at him without saying why. He decided that the pleasure he took in the girl's company was not worth the pain her absence gave him. One day he screwed up his courage, and told her so. *Hila hila*, she admitted to him that she felt exactly the same way. They decided to get married and live happily ever after. And that's the very end of the story. Just in time. Look, here comes your ma. She hates it when I tell you stories.

EPILOGUE

A MAN CALLED DOUGLAS was sitting with his back to his office desk, a child on his lap. He was middle-aged, dignified, pudgy, with sparse white hair. An American flag hung on the wall. Its bottom corners were unfastened and they blew in the breeze coming from a ceiling fan.

A woman in a simple blue jeans dress came in, handed him a white T-shirt, and pleaded, 'Here's a clean one. I already changed. I haven't worn a dress in years. Everyone is waiting. And stop telling that child all those fairy-tales. You are going to drive her nuts.' She took the child by the hand, and said, 'Cummon, Eliza, I need your help with the guests.'

When they had left, Douglas stood up, grumbling to himself. He changed into the fresh shirt, leaving the identical old one on the chair, and went outside. It was just past 9 a.m. on an August morning, when the sun in Nevada switches on like an oven. He stopped at an ice machine, and scooped up a handful of artificial snow. He squeezed the snow into a ball in his fist. When it had melted a little and

149

could be formed, he placed it as a wad at the back of his neck. It melted. He walked over to the gas-station office, his shirt dripping wet. The room was crowded with officials, and extra lights that had been brought in for the occasion.

A man in a city suit welcomed him.

'Douglas! We've come all the way out here to sing your praises and you run off and hide. You shy or something?'

'No, no,' he replied, speaking with an accent not native to that region, and which he always called, in answer to questions, 'an accent of unknown origin'. Douglas extended his hand. 'Welcome. My wife already welcomed you. I had to get myself ready. I'm feeling, I don't know, bashful maybe. It's . . . an honour.'

The official warmed to him, shook his hand with emotion.

'Bashful! I like that! I like that a lot. And you should be. This is not an everyday occurrence. I've come all the way from Winnetka, Jeff here has come from Seattle, Jerry from Kansas City, Piers and Nelson and Alan from New Haven – we travelled ourselves half to death to get here. Because we want you to be as proud of yourself as we are of you. Our company gives two medals a year, the Jim Smith Medal for productivity and the Joel Elliot prize for cleanest restrooms. It is the first time in our firm's history that we have awarded both medals to the same person. A fine man. Mr Douglas Allen.'

A camera flashed, wine glasses were pressed into hands, a video camera from a regional news station circled the room obnoxiously and a dozen voices cried, 'Speech! Speech!' Meanwhile, the small girl with black braids was darting about the adults until he picked her up, as if for his own comfort, and finally spoke into the microphone.

'Thank you. I don't know any fancy words to say thank you. I am a simple gas-station attendant, a small-time businessman, not a politician. I don't know how to give speeches like Terry does. But I know how to say thank you. So just let me say what I know how to say: thank you. Am I on television? I am?' He faced the video camera, took his daughter's hand and waved it, and called, 'Hello, America. Hello, everybody. And thank you. I love you.'

Everyone applauded and sang, 'For he's a jolly good fellow.' The music continued for a long time, and the hubbub was drawn out by the unveiling of a buffet with barbecued delicacies. No one saw the guest of honour leave the party, slip outside balancing a glass of wine. He passed a garage that held a series of cars, including a bright-yellow taxi, and continued to stroll towards the mountains, so similar to those of Turkish-Kurdistan, of central Nevada. The road ran straight towards the mountain range, passing a small building, a chapel. Behind this lay a pretty cemetery, with sagebrush and stone markers, some of them very old, some newer. He ambled towards the back of the cemetery until he found a particular gravestone. There he stood, and raising his glass to the tenant below the earth, he said, 'Noş.'